SOUL DEEP

by

Pamela Clare

SOUL DEEP

Published by Pamela Clare, 2015

Credits for cover images
Couple: PeopleImages.com
Landscape: Epic StockMedia/Depositphotos.com
Cover design by Carrie Divine/Seductive Designs
Copyright © 2015 by Pamela Clare

ISBN-10: 0990377121
ISBN-13: 978-0-9903771-2-2

DEDICATION

This book is dedicated to all the women—and men—who know that the human desire for romance, love, and sexual passion has nothing to do with age

ACKNOWLEDGEMENTS

This story would have been much more difficult to write if not for the unflagging support of the following wonderful people: my sister, Michelle White; my younger son, Benjamin Alexander; and my dear friends Jackie Turner, Shell Ryan, and Stéphanie Desprez. Thank you for your friendship and support.

Thanks, too, to Benjamin Gaibel, who helped me hold on when writing this book took me through my own personal loss and grief to a very dark place.

Special thanks and lots of love to Anette Stoltze, my dear friend from my teenage days at Sorø Akademi in Sorø, Denmark, and her husband, Erik Buhl, for taking me into their home and allowing me to experience life on their stud farm—Stutteri Brandtbjerggård in Pjested. By the time I'd been there for a week, I was the most relaxed I've been in years. Watching the birth of a colt and experiencing the workings of the farm was an incredible experience that I'll never forget. *Tusind tak!*

CHAPTER ONE

September 28

Janet Killeen gripped the steering wheel of her Toyota Corolla, snow falling so thick and heavy that she couldn't see the side of the highway. Her windshield wipers were clumped with ice and snow, the rubber blades no longer making contact with the glass. She would need to pull over soon to clean the ice off—if only she could see the shoulder so that she *could* pull over.

Leaving Denver had been a mistake.

She rolled down her window and scooted forward in her seat, ignoring the sharp pain that shot through her hip and pelvis at the motion. Reaching outside, she grabbed the bottom of the wiper blade. Icy flakes hit her face, the cold almost taking her breath away as she raised the blade and dropped it against her windshield once, twice, three times. The thick crust of ice and snow broke off.

She rolled up the window, turned her heater up a notch.

She'd left the city first thing this morning, hoping to make it to the mountain town of Scarlet Springs before the storm hit. She'd booked a room for a week at the Forest Creek Inn, a family-run bed and breakfast, and had been looking forward to seeing the aspens and maybe even sitting on a horse again. It was part of a promise she'd made herself, her way of celebrating her survival and the end of rehab.

Having grown up in Hudson Falls in upstate New York, she always yearned for fall color, and the only place a person could find that in Colorado was in the high country during that brief couple of weeks when the aspens turned. It had become her yearly ritual, the one time of year she put aside her badge and her duties as an FBI special agent and let herself go.

Forecasters had predicted up to eighteen inches in Denver and a good few feet in the mountains, but when were the forecasters ever right about Colorado's weather? Last week, they'd predicted snow, and Denver had gotten hail and funnel clouds instead. Of course, they just *had* to be right this time.

You should have turned back.

Yes, well, it was too late for that now. She needed to reach Scarlet Springs—or find someplace she could pull off the highway and wait for a break in the storm.

She glanced down at the speedometer. Ten MPH. At this rate, she'd get there faster if she got out of the car and ran. Except that she couldn't run. She would probably never run again. She was lucky to be able to walk.

You're lucky to be alive.

Last February, a sniper bullet intended for journalist Laura Nilsson, whose protection detail Janet had managed, had ripped through Janet's left hip, shattering the joint, breaking her pelvis, severing her sciatic nerve, and damaging her vaginal muscles before exiting through the front. Doctors had replaced her hip, used plates to put her pelvis back together, reconnected the severed nerve, and stitched her vagina, but her body would never be the same.

Gone were the days of running daily 10Ks and rock climbing on the weekends. Though she had learned to walk with a cane instead of a walker, her left foot still dragged. She didn't know whether she'd ever be able to ski or ride a horse or even enjoy sex again. Little things she'd always taken for granted were difficult now—grocery shopping, keeping a clean house, getting a full night of pain-free sleep.

And then there were the nightmares.

Gunshots. Screams. Pain.

That single bullet hadn't just ripped through her body. It had torn a path through her life. Byron, the skier she'd been dating, had ended things during her second month of rehab. He'd said that he'd changed and needed to move on, but she'd known he was turned off by her lack of mobility and had run out of patience waiting for them to have a sex life. But that wasn't all of it.

When she returned from this little vacation, she would be going back to work, but not to the position she'd held before the shooting. She'd be taking a desk job instead. An agent who couldn't run or stomach the thought of holding a firearm was an agent who couldn't leave the office.

The life she'd known had vanished in a split second, and she missed it, even grieved for it, crying tears she didn't share with anyone.

Melodie, her younger sister, saw this as a sign that Janet should leave the FBI, find a husband, and start a family before it was too late. Setting aside the fact that Janet's biological clock seemed to have run out already, her injuries would likely make sex and pregnancy difficult, even if by some miracle she could get pregnant.

Janet and Melodie were very different people. Melodie had always wanted to be a wife and a mother, and Janet had always wanted to be a superhero and save the world. It wasn't that Janet didn't want a husband or kids, but her life as a special agent had been busy and fulfilling enough without them. Besides, finding a husband wasn't like shopping for patio furniture. A woman could spend years looking for the right guy and still not find him. Janet had had her share of boyfriends and lovers, but after Byron, it seemed to her that a woman might be better off on her own.

Despite whatever her sister might think, Janet didn't regret her choices—not even her decision to volunteer for Laura's protection detail. She had always admired Laura and was proud to have played a role in saving her life. Laura had just married Javier Corbray, that sexy SEAL lover of hers. Seeing her move on from the hell that had been her life to claim some happiness had been the best reward Janet could have received.

She would adapt and find a way to do the things she loved again. That's exactly why she'd made this trip—to reclaim some part of her life for herself.

Snow had begun to build up on the wipers again, the tail lights of the truck that was at most ten feet in front of her barely visible. Janet rolled down her window once more, scooted forward, then grabbed the wiper blade and tapped it against the glass, dislodging the snow and ice.

It seemed to be coming down even harder now, the wind driving the snow straight into her windshield. How could the driver in front of her even see where he or she was going? Was the driver blindly following someone else's tail lights like she was? If so, what was guiding the person in front?

She needed to get off the road. She tried to remember if there were any gas stations or small towns between here and Scarlet Springs. She didn't think so. The only place she knew of for certain was the Cimarron Ranch, but she wouldn't stop there even if she knew where it was. Jack West, the man who owned it, was as big a jerk as he was handsome. She'd had a less-than-pleasant exchange with him when she'd gone there as part of Laura's protection detail to make certain the place was secured.

I know every man, woman, and child on my land, SA Killeen. I don't need you checking IDs or running background on my people. I understand you want to protect Ms. Nilsson. So do I. But I've got twenty men here, every single one of whom knows how to use a firearm. They've all been made aware of the situation. Laura is safe under my roof. I guarantee you that. Now, either come inside for a bite to eat, or get the hell off my property.

She'd only been trying to do her job, and West had ordered her off his land as if she'd been nothing more than a trespasser. She'd been furious at—

Ahead of her, the red tail lights swerved. The highway seemed to vanish from beneath her tires, the car sliding sideways down a steep embankment, coming to rest with a sickening *crunch.*

Janet found herself holding the steering wheel in a death grip, her heart slamming in her chest. She took a few deep breaths, tried to dial back on the adrenaline.

Way to go, Killeen. That's one way to get off the highway.

She wasn't hurt, and the car was no longer moving—two reasons to be grateful. The vehicle had come to rest at an almost forty-five-degree angle, what looked like a fencepost pressing against her crumpled passenger side door.

She knew there was no way for her to get back onto the road, not without trading her Corolla for, say, an M1 Abrams tank. She would have to call for help. The tow would probably cost a small fortune, to say nothing of the damage to her car and the fence.

Consider it all a tax on being stupid.

She turned off the vehicle, took off her seat belt, and bent down to retrieve her handbag off the floor. She pulled out her cell phone. No bars. "Damn it!"

She had no choice but to climb back up to the road. She might be able to flag down a trucker with a radio who could call for help on her behalf. Or maybe someone would come along who was willing to give her a ride to Scarlet Springs.

She grabbed her cane and pulled up the hood of her parka, determined not to be one of those drivers who wandered from their vehicles high in the mountains and froze to death in the snow. She pushed the door open— lifted it, really—then turned in her seat and tried to step out of the car into the snow. Her feet slipped, and she fell, instinctively reaching out with her hands to stop herself, her legs sliding beneath the car. The door swung down, almost hitting her in the face before she caught it.

Using her cane to steady herself and support her weight, she crawled out and got to her feet again, sidestepping the door and letting it slam behind her. Then she began to climb the embankment.

There couldn't have been more than twenty feet between her and the highway, but it might as well have been a mile. Last winter, she would have been able to do this without difficulty, but now it was a struggle. Again and again she slipped, gaining only a few feet despite intense effort, her thigh and hip aching, snow biting her face.

Swoosh!

A wave of white billowed down on her from above, knocking her backward down the embankment, losing her all the ground she'd gained.

Snow from a Colorado Department of Transportation snowplow.

Thanks a lot, CDOT.

Chilled to the bone, she shook off the snow, climbed to her feet, and tried again, this time setting her cane aside and attempting to crawl up the slope, dragging her left leg behind her. But the snow was too deep, and she was soon out of breath and badly chilled.

If she didn't stop, she'd soon be hypothermic.

By the time she was back in the car, she was exhausted, freezing, and in pain. She would have to wait here until the storm let up. When the snow stopped, she would wave out the window at passing drivers. Someone would see her and call for help. In the meantime, she had a space blanket, water, ibuprofen, her Kindle, and chocolate covered almonds. It wasn't the Forest Creek Inn, but it would have to do.

J ack West tossed the last hay bale into the bed of his Ford F-250 pickup, the cold biting his nose, the air fresh with the scent of new snow. A good four feet had fallen overnight, and the National Weather Service was saying the mountains could expect more this afternoon. He needed to get hay up to the herd in the high pasture before the flakes began to fly again.

He'd been working since before dawn, plowing the road to the ranch's front gate and then seeing to the horses. His son, Nate, normally took care of these things, but he'd stayed at the family townhome in Denver, not wanting to drive up the canyon with Megan, his wife, and Emily, their six-year-old daughter, in the middle of a blizzard. Jack supported that decision. He didn't like taking chances with the lives of those he loved.

Chuck, the ranch's foreman, stepped out of the barn. "Want me to come along?"

Jack frowned. "Is that your way of saying you think I'm too old for this shit?"

"You kidding, boss?" Chuck laughed. "You're in better shape than most of the younger guys."

"If that's true, I ought to fire the lot of you." Jack grinned, opened the cab door, and climbed into the driver's seat. "Did you take care of that business with Kip? I don't think ill of him, but I don't want him having the keys to the bunkhouse now that he's no longer working here."

Jack had found himself with no choice but to fire the man. Kip Henderson was a great cattleman, skilled with steers and horses, but he was also a slave to the bottle.

"I took care of it yesterday when Luke and I went into Denver to pick up supplies. His key is on my desk."

Jack shut the door, buckled the seatbelt. "I appreciate that."

Chuck stepped back to give the truck room. "See you when you get back."

Jack turned the key in the ignition, the 385-horsepower engine roaring to life. He headed down the road toward the main gate, his gaze traveling over the valley. Apart from his time in the army, he'd lived his entire life here, the third generation to call this mountain valley home. His family had done well, running black Angus and breeding quarter horses, managing to hang on through thick and thin to a way of life that had largely vanished from the state.

Jack turned up the truck's heater. The Cimarron had been transformed overnight into a landscape of frozen white, ribbons of golden aspen, dark patches of evergreens, and crags of red rock adding color to the mountainsides. The beauty of it was enough to take a man's breath away. Then the sun peered through the clouds on the eastern horizon, sending a shaft of pink light across the snow, making it sparkle.

Theresa, you would love this.

Whether Theresa could hear his thoughts, Jack couldn't say, but after almost forty years of being married to her, it was hard to experience life and not want to share it with her. She'd died seven years ago of a brain aneurysm, and Jack had never stopped missing her. One moment she'd been inside making lunch, and the next she'd been gone. He'd found her lying on the kitchen floor, and his world had come crashing down.

Still, life went on, and Jack had had no choice but to go on with it. When Nate had been wounded in Afghanistan, badly burned in an IED explosion, Jack had devoted himself to helping his son heal and regain his strength. Now Nate was happily married, his wife Megan and their little Emily bringing joy back into the house.

And if there were days—and nights especially—when Jack felt lonely, well, that was just the price he paid for the privilege of having lived so damned long.

Nate had given him his blessing to remarry and wanted him to join some online dating service, but Jack couldn't see how any good could come of that. Not that he didn't have anything to offer a woman. There was the ranch, of course, and he had money. And, unlike a lot of men his age, he was physically fit and didn't need a pill to get an erection. But he hadn't dated in forty years and wasn't sure he'd even know what to say to a woman.

Hell, no, that wasn't for him. He'd been married once and knew what it was to love a woman and be loved in return. He and Theresa had made a good life together, and they'd had a son. Now, she was gone, and Jack's job, as he saw it, was to be there for their son and his family and to pass on the Cimarron intact.

He reached the main gate, which he had already opened, and turned onto the highway. The road was slick and snow-packed—not surprising given how much accumulation they'd gotten. It was unusual for the state to get a blizzard this early in the fall, but this was Colorado. He'd seen it snow up here on the Fourth of July.

He was about a mile east of the turnoff to the high pasture when he saw a fencepost out of alignment with the others. It took a moment before he realized why the post had been knocked to the side. A car had slid off the road, down the embankment, and struck the fence. The car itself was all but buried in a big snowdrift, just a bit of tail light and rear bumper showing. CDOT plows must have buried it during the night, concealing it under a few feet of snow and slush.

Someone was going to have a fun time digging that out.

He drove to the access road and turned off the highway, stopping to lower the snowplow. It was slow going the rest of the way as he cleared the road. By the time he reached the pasture, the cattle were waiting for him.

He parked the truck, got out, and climbed into the bed, cutting the cords that bound the bales and tossing hay over the fence to the hungry animals, mostly pregnant cows. They jostled against one another, lowing, their breath sending up clouds of condensation.

"Mind your manners, ladies. Someone might think you were raised in a barn."

When he'd spread the hay out over the snow, he got back into his truck and headed home, his mind on a hot shower and strong coffee.

Bitch and moan though he might, he loved this life. Other people were out there right now fighting traffic on the highway so they could sit in offices all day doing bullshit work for other people, and he was out here, breathing mountain air, being his own boss, and doing the kind of work that left a man's body tired but his soul fulfilled.

Back on the highway, he made a mental note to repair that fencepost once the owner of the car had their vehicle towed. As he passed the car, he saw that the headlights were flashing. Was someone down there?

He pulled off onto the shoulder, parked, then called Chuck on his sat phone. "Hey, I'm on my way back. There's a car off the road just past mile marker one-thirty-three. I think someone's still in the vehicle. I'm going to check it out."

He turned on the truck's hazard lights and pocketed his keys, then climbed out of the pickup. Why anyone had gone out in yesterday's blizzard without all-wheel drive was beyond him. Didn't they realize they were in Colorado?

He grabbed a snow shovel out of the back, then crossed the road, snow squeaking under his boots. The slope was steep, and he slipped and slid his way down to the vehicle. A few minutes of shoveling, and he'd managed to unbury the driver's side window.

Through the frost-covered glass, he could just make out a woman's face.

She rolled down the window. "Jack West?"

He found himself looking into a pair of familiar green eyes. Her dark hair was longer than the last time he'd seen her, and there were lines of weariness on her face. Still, he recognized her immediately.

"Well, hello, there, SA Killeen. It seems you've run into a little trouble."

CHAPTER TWO

Janet stared up at him, unable to believe her bad luck. She'd only met him once, but she'd recognize him anywhere—those dark blue eyes, that square jaw, the thick salt-and-pepper hair, the dark brows, the rugged cheekbones.

Of all the fences along all the highways in the entire state of Colorado, she just *had* to crash into his.

Sluggish from cold and lack of sleep, she found herself explaining. "I ... I slid off the road yesterday morning. The truck in front of me swerved, and the next thing I knew ... Sorry about the fencepost."

She expected him to say something cutting or to make fun of drivers who didn't know how to handle the roads in snow, but he didn't.

"You've been down here since yesterday morning?"

"I tried to call for a tow, but ... "

He shook his head. "Your cell phone won't do you a damned bit of good here. Let's get you to my truck. Your car isn't going anywhere, I'm afraid."

She pushed aside the space blanket she'd wrapped herself in and reached for her cane, a wave of humiliation washing over her to think of him seeing her like this. "I ... I can't make it up the embankment. I tried."

She'd tried several times, but it was just too much for her left leg.

His gaze dropped to her cane, but he showed no surprise. He must have heard she'd been shot. "We'll figure it out. Can you stand?"

"Yes."

He opened the door and lifted it out of her way with one arm.

She turned in her seat so that both of her feet were out of the car, then slowly stood, her hip and pelvis screaming after yesterday's exertions and so many hours of immobility. She couldn't help the catch in her breath or keep herself from wincing.

"Easy does it. It's deep and slick out here." He caught her arm at the elbow.

The contact sent a strange awareness arcing through her, and she jerked her arm away so abruptly that she surprised even herself. She tried to think up an excuse. "I ... I need to grab my things."

"I'll come back for them. Let's just get you to the truck. I'm concerned that you might be hypothermic."

She couldn't argue with that. She'd been forced to turn off her engine and her heater with it when she'd realized that snow was blocking the tailpipe and she'd risk carbon monoxide poisoning if she left it running. The night had been bitter cold. "Okay."

He turned toward the embankment, put himself on her left side. "Why don't you wrap your arm around my shoulder? Let's try doing this three-legged-race style."

Cane in her right hand, she did as he'd suggested, then drew back, contact sending that same uncomfortable awareness through her. "Can't you just throw down a rope and pull me up?"

"You want me to winch you up like a cow?" The expression on his face told her that was *not* going to happen. "Come on. I won't bite. I promise."

"You did last time."

"Last time, you were playing federal agent on my land. This time, you're a stranded friend in need of my help."

That was news. "When did we become friends?"

He glared down at her. "If you want me to leave you here—"

"No! Please. Thank you." She put her arm around his shoulder.

He caught her around the waist. "Step off on your right foot."

She took a step, felt herself begin to slide.

Strong arms steadied her, kept her from slipping. "Don't put weight on your left leg. Let me do the work on this side."

She hopped, his arms holding her fast, his boots gripping the snow, the embankment so steep that if she had leaned out, she would almost have been able to touch it.

Hop. Hop. Hop.

Slowly, they moved upward. She didn't know if it was exhaustion or the cold or the altitude, but it was hard work, her left foot dragging in the snow.

Hop. Hop. Hop.

"That's it. We're almost there."

"I have to stop." Janet had been a track champion in high school and college. She wasn't used to feeling so weak—or needing anyone's help.

He wasn't breathing hard at all. "There's no rush. My truck won't go anywhere without us."

She fought to catch her breath, her heartbeat slowly returning to normal, the icy air burning her lungs. She found herself leaning against him and jerked herself upright. "I'm good to go."

Hop. Hop. Hop.

Up they climbed, Jack somehow managing to keep the two of them from slipping, his body moving with the confidence and agility of a man who'd lived his entire life in the outdoors.

The low growl of a diesel engine and the scrape of a plow on the road announced the approach of another CDOT plow.

"Oh, great." Janet had heard that sound many times during the night, each pass resulting in another wave of snow that had buried her deeper. "Get ready."

"Shit." In a single move, Jack pivoted to stand in front of her, turned his back to the road, and drew her against him, using his body to shield her from the brunt of the snow and slush that rained down on them. "Damned idiots."

She looked up at him, her head filled with his scent—pine, fresh air, a hint of spicy shaving cream. "Thanks."

He took his place at her side again. "Ready?"

Hop. Hop. Hop. Hop. Hop.

And then they were at the top of the embankment, the road an icy ribbon between them and Jack's pickup.

Again Janet had to stop. "Please … I just … have to… catch my breath."

With no warning, Jack scooped her off her feet and into his arms.

She gave a little shriek. "What—?"

"I've got you." He crossed the highway and went around the back of the truck to the passenger side door. Somehow he managed to open it, then lifted her into the seat. "I'll be right back."

In another few minutes, he returned with her suitcase and handbag, stowing the former in the back of the cab and handing her the latter, before climbing into the driver's seat. "Where were you headed?"

He started the engine, merged back onto the highway.

"I have a reservation for a week at the Forest Creek Inn in Scarlet Springs. I wanted to see the aspens."

"We can call them from the ranch, let them know you're okay. I know Bob and Kendra Jewell. They'll be worried about you."

"You're... you're taking me to the Cimarron?" She'd thought he'd been offering to take her to Scarlet Springs.

"Scarlet Springs is a good two hours up the road, and there's more snow in the forecast. I can't see it would do you any good to be up there without your vehicle. How would you get back? Besides, I doubt you're up for the drive."

It was on the tip of her tongue to tell him that she didn't want to go to his damned ranch, but she knew he was right. She wasn't up for the drive, and if he did take her to Scarlet Springs, she'd be stuck there.

"We'll get you fed, warm you up, and you can get some sleep. I can't imagine it was comfortable sitting in that car for 24 hours."

Was this the same Jack West she'd met last February?

"Why are you being so nice?"

He glanced over at her. "I know our first meeting was confrontational, but let's just say you don't know me very well if you think I'd let a woman who's cold, hungry, tired, and in obvious pain deal with this situation by herself. If that's not good enough for you, then know that my family owes you a great debt. Javier Corbray is my son's best friend. He dragged Nate out of a burning vehicle in Afghanistan and saved his life. That makes him and his bride, Laura Nilsson, family."

"I see." Because that sounded cold and ungrateful, she added, "Thank you."

"You're welcome."

The truck's heater pumped delicious warm air through the cab. Within minutes, she found herself fighting to stay awake. It couldn't have been more than a half an hour when they turned off the highway and another five minutes after that when the ranch house appeared in the distance. The sight of it roused her from her stupor.

It was even more beautiful than she'd remembered. Its steep, multiple gables made her think of Swiss chalets, while the stone and log construction was western. Several stone chimneys rose up from the roof, dozens of windows stretching skyward, making her think of European cathedrals, the glass reflecting the mountains that surrounded them. The front door was set back from a portico driveway that was accented by a colonnade of polished logs. Off to the west stood several corrals and large outbuildings, including what looked like a riding hall.

"It's beautiful."

Jack smiled. "My grandfather bought the land to run cattle. My father took over from him. He expanded the holdings, added horse breeding, built most of the outbuildings. Theresa and I rebuilt the house."

Janet had just assumed the West family was made of money and had bought the ranch recently—a mountain trophy house. She hadn't realized it was part of a true ranching legacy. "Is Theresa your wife?"

"Yes—or she was. She passed on about seven years ago."

Janet didn't miss the note of sadness in his voice. She hadn't meant to tread on sensitive ground. "I'm sorry."

Jack drove the pickup to the side of the house and pulled into the five-car garage. By the time he'd climbed out and reached the passenger side, Janet had already opened her door and begun to climb down, her right foot reaching for the concrete.

He took her arm, steadied her. "I'll bring in your stuff. You just head inside where it's warm. The kitchen's through there."

He grabbed her suitcase out of the cab and followed her in through the mudroom, where he stopped to take off his wet boots before moving on again.

"I'll set you up in the guest room. You can take a hot shower or lie down and rest while I make us some lunch and coffee." He led her down the hallway and put her in the room next to his. It was the only guestroom that wouldn't force her to use the stairs. He set her suitcase down and turned up the thermostat. "You've got your own bathroom. It's got radiant heat. Turn the thermostat up as high as you like. Towels are in the cupboard. There's a landline on the nightstand if you need to make calls."

"Wow. This is amazing."

"Make yourself at home, SA Killeen."

"Janet." She sat on the bed. "It's Janet."

"I'll have lunch ready in thirty minutes, Janet—unless you'd rather sleep."

Those green eyes went wide. "Oh, no, please. I'm starving."

"Let me know if you need anything." He turned and left her in peace, then made his way back to the mudroom, where he finally slipped off his wet parka and hung it on its hook before putting his boots on the boot dryer.

Back in the kitchen, he washed his hands, then got last night's leftover chili out of the refrigerator, dumped it in a pot, and turned the burner on low, the spicy scent sparking his hunger. He'd made a big batch yesterday afternoon, only to find out that Nate and the girls would be staying in

Denver. Now the extra would make for a solid lunch, and it would taste even better than it had last night.

Jack liked it when things balanced themselves like that, the chaos and asymmetries of life coming together in surprising ways to achieve order.

While the chili reheated, he mixed up a batch of cornbread, popped it into the oven, then set the table. He'd never cooked when Theresa was alive. For a time after her death, he'd survived off frozen meals and whiskey. But with his wife gone and Nate downrange fighting Al Qaeda, · Jack had realized he either needed to learn to cook or get used to being hungry and drunk. To his surprise, he'd discovered he enjoyed cooking.

He had a few minutes, so he called the Forest Creek Inn and told Bob Jewell what had happened, then called Chuck to let him know he was back. "I don't know how we're going to get her car out of there, but we won't worry about that now."

He hung up, heard the tap of her cane on the floor, and glanced over his shoulder to see her enter the kitchen. She walked with a pronounced limp, her left foot dragging, but that's not what held his attention.

Damn, she was pretty.

Her dark hair was still damp, hanging below her shoulders in wet tendrils. She wore no makeup, her face perfect without it. She'd put on a pair of gray leggings and a white angora sweater that clung a bit too nicely to her curves. Even standing over a pot of chili, he could smell the clean scent of her shampoo.

Back off, West, you old goat!

She was young enough to be his daughter, for God's sake. She couldn't be much older than Nate—late thirties, maybe early forties—and he was sixty-three. His mind had no business heading off in that direction, even if she had felt mighty sweet in his arms when he'd carried her.

"Better?"

She nodded. "Yes, thank you. That smells incredible."

"Leftover chili." He lifted the lid, stirred the pot. "Have a seat. As soon as the cornbread is done, we'll be ready to eat. What can I get you to drink?"

She winced as she sat. "Coffee with milk would be great. Thank you."

It was a damned shame that she'd been wounded at such a young age. She would have to deal with this for the rest of her life, just like Nate had to cope with his burns. Sometimes life was brutally unfair.

He poured her a cup of coffee, set it with the milk on the table, then busied himself serving lunch, getting the chili into bowls, pulling the cornbread out of the oven, putting a couple of thick wedges on plates, setting the butter crock on the table. When the meal was served, he sat across from her. "Dig in."

She took a bite of the chili, then stared at him in surprise. "This is really good."

"Damned straight it is. I'd feign modesty, but why bother?"

That made her smile, little dimples appearing in her cheeks. "Is it an old family recipe?"

He'd never seen her smile before, and the effect had his pulse skipping. "You could say that. I've made a few changes over the years. Bourbon is my secret ingredient. After Theresa died, I found that cooking with her recipes made her seem closer."

Janet's delicate brow bent in a frown. "I can understand that. My parents died when I was five. My grandparents raised my sister and me."

"I'm sorry to hear that." Jack thought of his precious little Emily and how hard it would be for her if Nate and Megan were somehow killed. It made his heart ache. He pushed the thought away. "It's a hell of a thing to lose someone you love."

"Yes, it is." Janet ate the rest of her meal with the unselfconscious gusto of the truly hungry, polishing off her bowl of chili in silence, then eating the slice of cornbread. "Would you mind if I have seconds?"

"No, I would not mind." He stood, picked up her bowl, and refilled it. "You may have thirds and fourths, too, if you like. There's plenty."

She ate the second bowl more slowly, stopping to sip her coffee. It wouldn't be long before exhaustion took over.

"You said you were heading up to Scarlet Springs to see the aspens."

She nodded, held the coffee cup between her palms as if to warm her fingers. "It's an annual ritual of mine, one of the few times I get out of the city. I'd been hoping to do some horseback riding, too. It's one of my favorite—*was* one of my favorite escapes. I'm not sure I can still manage it."

"You'll find a way." That gave Jack an idea. "You know, we've got aspens, and we've got horses and a riding hall. Why don't you spend your week here? It's free. The accommodations are first rate. The food is terrific, if I do say so myself. And we won't have to worry about getting you up to Scarlet Springs and back."

Had he really invited her to spend a week under his roof?

Sure, he had. And why not?

Weren't guests the entire point of having this big damned house?

She dabbed her lips with her napkin, her gaze averted. "Thanks for the invitation, but I really couldn't impose. It was kind of you to help me out and give me a place to stay the night, but tomorrow I'll call a towing company and get out of your hair."

It was on his tongue to tell her that he kind of liked having her in his hair, but that felt like tipping his hand. "Suit yourself."

This is what he got for acting in such a charming manner the first time they'd met.

Well, hell.

She set her napkin down, her gaze traveling from her bowl to the dishes in the sink. "I'll help you clean up."

"No, ma'am, absolutely not." He stood, piled her bowl onto his, carried them to the sink. "I've got it. You go and rest. I'll have dinner ready at about six, barring any bovine or equine catastrophes. You can join me or sleep, whichever works for you."

She reached for her cane and carefully got to her feet. "Thanks so much. It really was delicious."

"You're welcome. Get some rest."

He set the dishes in the sink and watched as she slowly walked away.

CHAPTER THREE

Janet opened her eyes, glanced around, tried to remember where she was. The Forest Creek Inn? No, she'd never made it there. She'd gone off the road and...

She was at the Cimarron.

Jack West of all people had found her and brought her here.

She sat up, rubbing her hip, her mind sluggish from hours of deep sleep and the single Percocet she'd allowed herself to take. Outside, it was still light. She pushed the illuminator button on her watch and saw that it was just after five PM.

She reached over, turned on the bedside lamp, and looked at her surroundings. She'd been so exhausted earlier that she hadn't really noticed how beautiful the guest room was. Someone had clearly put effort into making it cozy and comfortable.

The sleigh bed she was lying in was almost certainly an antique, leaves and scrollwork carved into a headboard and footboard of polished cherry. The white quilt that had kept her warm was covered with colorful appliqué flowers, delicate vines and leaves curled artfully around the blossoms—violets, roses, tulips, irises, daffodils. She didn't have to look closely to know it was hand-pieced like the quilts her grandmother used to make. A stone fireplace stood against one wall, its wooden mantle

decorated with family photos. Deep red draperies framed a single wide
window, the white blinds lowered, diffusing what little daylight remained.
A baker bench sat at the foot of the bed, upholstered in velvet the same
color as the draperies. An antique chest of drawers that matched the bed sat
beneath a watercolor painting of snow-capped mountains.

The room was every bit as lovely as anything she might have gotten at
the bed and breakfast. Then she remembered the bathroom.

She reached for her cane, got out of bed, her hip and thigh stiff but no
longer hurting. She crossed the room, reached inside the bathroom, and
flicked on the lights, a little sigh leaving her at the sight.

The heated stone floor was warm against her feet as she stepped
inside, taking it all in—the marble counters, the two oval sinks, the multi-
head shower surrounded by glass walls. But what delighted her most was
the soaking tub. Deep and wide, it sat beneath a delicate chandelier, a little
piece of paradise.

She *had* to take a long, hot bath before she left the ranch.

That's when she remembered that Jack had invited her to stay for the
week. The offer was tempting—and not only because of the tub. The man
himself had more than his share of appeal.

She found it hard not to forgive him for their first encounter after he'd
done so much for her today. Good lord, he'd actually scooped her off her
feet and carried her to his pickup. No man had ever carried her. At five-
foot-nine, she was tall for a woman, but Jack was taller. Beneath his down
parka, he was all muscle. Being held like that had made her feel small,
feminine.

Stop it, Killeen.

The man wasn't interested in her. He'd carried her because he'd
known she was exhausted and because they'd needed to cross the highway

quickly, not because he found her irresistible. Even if he did, she didn't want to complicate her already complicated life any further by getting involved with a man right now.

She looked in the mirror. There were dark circles beneath her eyes, and her hair was a tangled mess. She reached for her brush, ran it through her hair, then retrieved her makeup bag. She did her best to conceal the dark circles and make herself look alive—a little eyeliner, some mascara, a touch of blush.

Then again, it didn't matter how she looked. She wasn't trying to impress anyone—or she shouldn't be.

She put on the same clothes she'd worn at lunchtime and, remembering that dinner would be ready at about six, left her room and walked back down the hallway, the sound of classical music drifting toward her from the kitchen. But when she reached the end of the hallway, she stopped and stared.

Jack West's home was stunning, with timbered, vaulted ceilings, floor-to-ceiling windows that looked out onto the mountains, an enormous fireplace of rounded river stones in the living room, a formal dining area with a table that could easily seat a dozen people, and a wide stairway that led to more rooms upstairs.

"Want a tour?" Jack stood in the doorway to the kitchen, watching her, a denim apron over a black turtleneck and jeans. "We don't need to go upstairs. There's not much up there besides bedrooms."

"I'd like that." She followed him while he showed her his office, with its masculine leather furniture and neat bookshelves; the gym with its sauna and the hot tub they'd just installed; a breathtaking two-story library that had its own fireplace; the home theater; and, last but not least, the wine cellar.

Janet struggled not to look amazed by it all. She'd had no idea cattle ranching could be so lucrative. Or maybe it wasn't the cattle. Maybe it was the horses. Regardless, the Cimarron was like no place she'd ever seen.

Jack turned toward the wall of wines. "This reminds me. We need something for dinner. How about a nice cru Beaujolais?" He drew a bottle from the rack and read off the name in French. "Côte de Brouilly from Château Thivin. This ought to do."

"You're an oenophile?"

He frowned. "Does that surprise you?"

Janet's mind was still muddled by Percocet. That's the only explanation for the words that came out of her mouth next—and the flirty tone of voice she used when she said them. "A lot of things I've learned about you today surprise me."

Jack's lips curved slowly into a smile that made her pulse skip. "Is that so?"

Jack poured wine into Janet's glass, fighting to ignore what felt suspiciously like nerves. "Bon appétit."

What the hell did he possibly have to be nervous about?

Absolutely nothing. That's what.

This wasn't a date or some damned romantic liaison. He was having dinner with an acquaintance who'd gotten stranded near his property—and who just happened to be a beautiful woman. She probably had a boyfriend or, hell, maybe a girlfriend.

She smiled, those dimples appearing again. "It smells delicious."

Not sure what she liked, he'd decided to keep dinner simple—a roast chicken, buttered new potatoes with parsley, an arugula salad, green beans, and rolls.

"Thanks." He sat, spread a cloth napkin on his lap. "We trade with a friend of ours—organic free-range beef for organic free-range birds."

She raised her glass. "Cheers."

He raised his. "Cheers."

They drank.

"This is very good." Janet looked at the wine, took another sip. "I don't know as much about wine as I should, but I do appreciate a good wine when I taste it. My mother's parents made their own wine from grapes they grew themselves. They grew most of what we ate."

"You grew up on a farm?" Now it was his turn to be surprised. He'd had her figured for a big-city type.

"My grandfather grew apples, so it was really more of an orchard than a farm, though they did have a big vegetable garden. My grandmother canned everything. We had chickens and beehives, too. I helped her with the chickens—when I wasn't too busy running wild."

While they ate, Jack listened to Janet talk about her childhood, her voice smooth and melodic, her green eyes taking on a sparkle. He tried to envision the woman who'd shown up at the ranch last February wearing a stiff pantsuit, a gun, and a badge as a little girl who'd eaten fresh honey from a hive, helped her grandma gather eggs, played hide and seek in the barn, and climbed into apple trees to read books.

"They had sugar maples on the property, so every spring we'd tap the trees to gather the sap and then boil it down to make maple syrup, maple butter, and maple candy. I miss that here. No one in Colorado has even heard of maple cream pie."

"I can't say I've heard of it myself." But Jack would damned well look it up. He liked a challenge. "Is that where you learned to ride?"

She took a sip of her wine, nodded. "They had two dressage horses—Hanoverian geldings. I was riding horses before I could walk, or so I've been told."

As a rule, Jack didn't go in for woo-woo, but he'd swear there was a spiritual connection between women and horses. He'd seen it often enough to believe it was real. He'd always thought women were more in tune with their bodies and with nature than most men. Maybe there was an earthiness in women that connected with the wildness in horses. Hell, how should he know?

"My Nate was sitting in a saddle when he was still in diapers." Jack set his fork aside, his plate clean. "I'll show you the stables tomorrow—unless you're dead set on getting out of here."

She smiled, a warm flush in her cheeks from the wine. "I think I can stay that long. I would love to see your horses."

"So how did a farm girl from upstate New York end up becoming an FBI agent?" He poured the last of the wine into their glasses.

Her smile faded, and the sparkle left her eyes. "My parents were murdered."

Her words hit Jack square in the face. "Murdered?"

She nodded, drank the last of her wine. "They put a classified ad in the paper to sell their old car. A man called and said he wanted to come by and see it. When my dad went outside to show him the vehicle, the bastard shot him in the chest. My mother was making supper. She heard the shot and ran outside to help my dad. The SOB shot her, too, then backed over her while she was still alive and drove off with the car. I was five. Melodie, my sister, was three. I'm not sure what we were doing—playing in our bedroom or something. A neighbor saw the whole thing and called the police. It was the FBI who tracked him down and brought him in."

"Was he convicted?"

She shook her head. "They found him dead in his cell. Apparently, he picked a fight with the wrong people and got shanked."

The bastard had damned well deserved it.

"I'm sorry." Jack reached over, took her hand, held it. "I can't imagine how hard it was for you and your sister."

He couldn't imagine how difficult it had been for her grandparents, either—losing their daughter and son-in-law and then having to explain death to two tiny children who suddenly depended on them for everything.

"Thanks." Janet gave him a tight smile that didn't reach her eyes, drew her hand away. "The FBI agents who came to speak with my grandparents seemed like heroes to me. I knew that I wanted to do what they did when I grew up."

"Catch bad guys?"

She nodded. "Catch bad guys—and keep good people from being hurt."

"I hope it brings you some peace to know you've managed to do exactly that." He raised his glass. "Here's to you."

"Thanks." She smiled again, but he could see the sadness in her eyes. "That's kind of you to say."

"Nonsense." Jack didn't have a kind bone in his body. "It's the truth."

As he finished his wine, he found himself wishing he'd been a little more cooperative and a little less brusque the first time she'd been here.

After dinner, they moved into the living room, where Jack lit a roaring fire in the fireplace and opened a second bottle of wine.

"Oh, I couldn't." Janet shook her head. Then again, why shouldn't she? The Percocet she'd taken after lunch had worn off, and it had only been a single pill. Besides, it wasn't often that she got to taste wine of this quality. "Okay, but just one more glass."

Jack filled their glasses, then carried his to the other end of the sofa and sat. "You warm enough?"

"Yes. Thank you." She took another sip, savoring the vibrant, earthy fruit taste of the Beaujolais. "You know a lot more about me than I know about you."

He shrugged. "There's not a lot to know."

She couldn't help but smile. "I thought you didn't believe in false humility."

"Okay, but don't blame me when your eyes glaze over. I grew up on the ranch, an only child. I married my high school sweetheart after graduation, then joined the army and served six years with the Army Rangers—long-range reconnaissance patrol, Company H, 75th Infantry." His eyes took on a far-away look. "I did two tours of duty in Vietnam. We lost a lot of good men. That was a long time ago. Most Americans don't know anything about it."

Janet hated to admit it, but she knew very little about Vietnam. She would make a point of rectifying that. "What did you do when you got back?"

"I came home to Theresa and the Cimarron. Nate was born a few years later. He was our only child. That's not what we wanted, but it's what happened. Theresa had a few miscarriages after he was born, and then it just became too difficult for her. We stopped trying."

Janet could understand that. "I'm sorry. That must have been very hard."

"Life is what it is. We had a lot of good years together, and I'm grateful for that."

Even though he sat at the other end of the sofa, she was keenly aware of him, the deep, soothing sound of his voice, his masculine scent.

"Why haven't you remarried?" The moment the words left her mouth, she wished she could take them back. "I'm sorry. It's none of my business. You loved your wife very much. I realize you can't just turn that off."

Stop while you're behind, Killeen!

"I loved her very much." He looked down at his wine glass, then into her eyes. "I might remarry—if the right woman were to come along. But what are the chances? An old guy like me? I'm sixty-three, past the age for dating."

"Give me a break!" Janet laughed. "You helped me up that embankment today without breaking a sweat, then carried me to your truck like I weighed nothing. Those are hardly the actions of an 'old guy.'"

His gaze was fixed on hers, his blue eyes dark. "That's kind of you to say."

"It's not kind at all. You're a very handsome man, Jack West. I think any woman would look at you and think that."

It dawned on her that perhaps she was giving too much away, but the wine and the look in his eyes made that worry unravel.

"So, tell me, SA Killeen, do you have a significant other? That's the term in modern parlance, isn't it?"

She couldn't help but laugh. "Yes, it is, and, no, I don't."

She found herself telling him about Byron and the way he'd left her, only leaving out the part about her torn vaginal muscles. "I was told I needed to avoid sex for a while, and that was just too much for him in the end. That's not the excuse he gave me, but I'm sure that was the last straw."

Usually when she thought about that last conversation with Byron, she found herself fighting tears, the pain almost as fresh as it had been the day he'd left. But at this moment, she was more aware of the anger that flashed in Jack's eyes.

"What a goddamned asshole! He did you a favor by getting the hell out of your life." Jack frowned, his expression turning apologetic. "Sorry. My mouth gets ahead of me. I talk before I think. I'm sure it was very painful to lose him on top of everything else you were dealing with at the time."

It had been, but somehow Jack's rage on her behalf helped her feel better.

"It's okay, and you're right. He really *did* do me a favor." She hadn't thought of it that way before.

"Nate faced a similar situation." He told her how Nate had been badly burned in an IED explosion in Afghanistan and then flown to San Antonio, where he'd spent weeks fighting for his life. "I flew down to be with him. His fiancée came to visit, too. I thought she was there to show her support. Instead, she broke it off. He was lying there, suffering ungodly pain and facing dozens of surgeries, and she broke off their engagement."

Janet didn't hold back. "What a bitch!"

It wasn't a word she used lightly.

Jack nodded. "You've got that right. But, in the end, she did him a favor. He's got a good woman now, one who loves him because of the man he is—not despite his scars, but *because* of them."

"He's a lucky man." The sharp edge of loneliness cut through the warm buzz of the wine.

"What I'm saying is that you'll find a man who loves you like that—a man who loves and respects you because of your courage, not despite your injury and the physical challenges you face."

She liked what he'd said, sweet words she wished she could believe, but she had to be honest. "I'm not as brave as you think I am. I haven't been able to pick up a firearm since the day I was shot."

"Anyone who tells you you're not brave because you won't pick up a gun hasn't experienced a fire-fight first hand." There was understanding in his eyes.

She'd needed to hear that so very badly, but his compassion didn't change the rest of it. "The kind of men I'm attracted to—athletic, outdoorsy guys—want women who can keep up with them. Besides, I'm forty-five."

"You don't look a day over thirty-eight." He gave her a devastatingly sexy smile. "And, hey, if an old codger like me can't play the age card, then neither can you."

She couldn't help but laugh. "It's different for men. You know that."

"You're a beautiful woman." The way he said it made her breath catch.

Warmth rushed into her cheeks. "Is that you talking—or the Côte de Brouilly?"

"It takes more than a few glasses of wine to make me say things I don't mean—scotch if you want poetry." He moved closer, took their wine glasses, and set them down on the coffee table. "Janet…"

His words trailed into silence. Then he leaned in and kissed her. His lips were soft and warm as they brushed lightly over hers, their caress an invitation.

Her pulse skipped. "*Jack.*"

Heat that had nothing to do with the wine slid into her blood. She rested her palms against the hard wall of his chest and kissed him back, brushing her lips over his, nipping his upper lip, then tracing the fullness of his lower lip with her tongue, her senses aroused by the taste of him, by the scent of his skin, by the hardness of his body.

He caught the tip of her tongue between his teeth, the intensity in his dark eyes making her belly flutter. Then his eyes drifted shut. One strong arm encircled her waist, drawing her against him, while his other hand slid into her hair to angle her head. Then his mouth closed over hers in a deep, slow kiss.

Oh, yes.

Her eyes closed, too, both of them going by feel now. She parted her lips, let him take the lead. The man knew how to kiss, his fingers tracing her spine, sending shivers through her, his tongue teasing hers, his lips firm and insistent.

This is how she'd always wanted to be kissed, and, God, he'd better not stop anytime soon because she wanted more.

CHAPTER FOUR

Jack drew Janet closer, the physical contact making his heart pound, his very blood seeming to come alive. It had been so long since he'd touched a woman, so long since he'd kissed a woman. At first, he was afraid he might have forgotten how, but then her arms locked behind his neck, pulling him closer, and he figured he must be doing something right.

God, she tasted sweet, her body soft and pliant in his arms. He raised the stakes, let his tongue have its way with hers. She gave a little whimper, arching so that her breasts pressed against his chest.

And damned if his jeans didn't feel uncomfortably tight.

They ought to stop.

Then again, why the hell should they? They were both adults. She seemed to know what she wanted, and so did he.

There came a knock at the mudroom door, Chuck's voice calling to him. "Hey, boss, there's a problem with Chinook."

Damn it to hell!

"I'm sorry. That's Chuck, my foreman. He wouldn't bother me at this hour unless it was serious." Jack ran a thumb down Janet's cheek, then called out to Chuck. "I'll be right there, damn it!"

"Can I come?" Janet's cheeks were flushed, her lips swollen and wet.

God, how he wished Nate were here to handle the horses. Then again, if his son were here, Jack probably wouldn't be making out on the sofa like a teenager.

"I don't see why not." He stood, helped her to her feet. "You'll need to get bundled up. It will be a snowy walk to the stables, but it's not far."

"I'll get my coat."

"I'll meet you out there."

He watched her walk away, cane tapping softly on the wooden floor, then headed to the mudroom, where Chuck was waiting for him.

"Luke is calling Doc Johnson, but you're going to want to see this yourself. Chinook has been shot in the forearm."

"What the hell?" Jack's adrenaline spiked.

"Burt brought him in at dusk but didn't notice anything. Luke went to settle him with hay for the night. He called me in, and I saw what looks like a graze wound on his left forearm."

"How the hell could Burt miss something like that?" Jack wasn't pleased.

"I don't know. We're guessing that hunting party didn't move on the way you asked them to, and someone fired a shot that ricocheted or got caught in the wind."

"I thought you told me they'd cleared camp." Jack couldn't abide trespassers.

Every summer and fall, he had to deal with people who came onto his property without permission to fish and hunt. He and his men chased them away, the sight of a dozen armed men usually enough to make them leave.

"Their camp was gone. Could be they just moved and set up a new one."

"Could be. Did anyone hear the shot?"

Chuck shook his head. "No."

Jack put on his boots, slipped into his parka, and grabbed his gloves. "Shovel a path from the house to the stables, and make sure Ms. Killeen makes it safely. I don't want her slipping."

"You got it, boss."

Jack stepped outside. The wind had kicked up, icy snowflakes biting his face. The stars and mountaintops were hidden behind dark clouds. More snow was coming.

Inside the heated barn, he found Luke still on the phone with Doc Johnson, a woolen ski cap covering his red hair. "He's right here."

"Thanks, Luke." Jack took the phone. "Sorry to trouble you, Doc. I haven't had a chance to look at the wound myself. We'll call you back in five. If it's something we can handle, we will. I don't want you coming out in this weather unless it's a true emergency."

Doc Johnson had been their vet for close to twenty years and had become a friend of the family. He'd forgotten more about horses than most people would ever know.

Jack walked back to Chinook's stall, found him stomping nervously, his muscular body shuddering.

"He seems pretty shook up," Luke said.

Jack called to Chinook and was relieved when the big animal came to greet him. "Hey, boy, what's going on?"

He rubbed the stallion's soft muzzle, spoke quietly to him, tried to calm him, then entered his stall, sliding the door closed behind him.

Immediately he saw the wound—a deep graze across the animal's upper left forearm. Blood still oozed from the gash, trails of dried blood running down his leg. How could Burt have missed this? Had the man been sleepwalking?

"Has anyone checked the corral for evidence?" If they knew what angle the shot had come from, Jack might be able to take a few men out on snowmobiles and confront the bastards who'd done this.

Luke shook his head. "I don't think so, boss."

"I'd like to know where he was standing when he was hit. There ought to be some sign—blood on the snow or something." Jack was about to send Luke out to search, but the kid was new and might unknowingly step on something. "Trade places with Chuck. He's shoveling snow. Send him to me. I want him on this."

Luke looked like he wanted to object but wisely changed his mind. "You got it."

Jack attached cross ties to the stallion's halter and clipped them to the sides of the stall. He needed to keep the horse still so he could examine the wound. Chinook didn't seem to be favoring the leg, so the bone couldn't be broken.

Thank God for that.

It would break Jack's heart to have to put Chinook down.

He heard voices and looked over to see Chuck walk in with Janet.

"Oh, wow!" Janet stared at the stallion like a woman who'd just fallen in love.

"How's he doing, boss?"

"It looks like the bone is okay, but I need to clean the wound and get a closer look. Can you get on the phone with Doc Johnson and tell him we can handle this ourselves? It looks like flakes are about to fly, and I don't want him risking the drive. When you're done with that, grab a flashlight and get out to the corral. I want to know where he was standing when he was hit."

"On it." Chuck turned and walked away.

Janet walked up to the grill, reached through the bars to rub Chinook's muzzle. "He's beautiful. I love palominos."

The stallion gave a soft whicker.

"It's nice to meet you, too," Janet answered. "I'm so glad you're okay."

Jack pointed to the wound. "You can see here on his forearm—a three-inch contusion. It's pretty deep. I don't think it could be anything but a bullet graze. It seems to have stopped bleeding on its own, but I'd like to clean it and get a closer look."

He stepped out of the stall, closed the door. "Why don't you two get acquainted while I get the first aid supplies?"

"That sounds like a good idea, doesn't it, buddy?" Janet answered, speaking more to Chinook than to Jack.

Yep. Women and horses.

Janet held Chinook's halter, while Jack irrigated the wound with sterile saline, then washed it with an antiseptic soap and rinsed it. When the blood was washed away, he probed the wound gently with gloved fingers. She couldn't help but admire his skill or the gentle way he handled the big animal.

Had she really just been kissing him?

Yes, she had, and he'd been skilled at that, too. She'd enjoyed every second of it, her lips still tingling, her body still warm from being pressed so closely against his.

"We're damned lucky. It's just a flesh wound. It should heal well, but it's likely to form proud flesh if we don't stay on top of it. I'm going to get some tea tree oil on here and then bandage him up."

"Tea tree oil?" She'd never heard of using that on a horse before.

Jack got to his feet. "It's got antimicrobial properties but isn't cytotoxic the way iodine and hydrogen peroxide are. Doc Johnson, our vet, is an old hippie. He swears by the natural shit, and so far he hasn't steered us wrong. If he prescribed butterflies and rainbows, I'd go for it."

Janet couldn't help but laugh. "He sounds like a character."

Jack opened the door to the stall. "Do you feel safe staying in here with him? He's very high spirited."

The question surprised her. It hadn't occurred to her to be afraid of the stallion. "Yes. No worries. We'll be fine."

He grinned, nodded, the warmth in his blue eyes making her pulse skip. "I'll be back in a few."

He stepped out, shut the stall door behind him, and walked away.

Janet patted the stallion's powerful neck. "Who did this to you, boy?"

Had it been hunters like Jack and his men suspected?

The horse whickered, watched her with a dark eye.

She hadn't allowed herself to look at the wound yet, not directly. But now that she was alone with Chinook in his stall, she glanced down. The wound was nothing like the one that had torn through her hip and pelvis, but it was clearly a bullet wound, cutting through the fleshy part of the stallion's upper forearm.

Sniper! Nine o'clock!

Bullets. Screaming. Pain.

Chinook jerked on the reins, pulling her back to the moment. The big animal clearly sensed her distress, and it made him nervous.

She drew a deep breath into her lungs, willed herself to focus on the stallion and the present moment. "Sorry, buddy."

She saw a blue rubber curry comb resting on the inside ledge of the grill. She released Chinook's halter and walked over to retrieve it, the thick layer of straw making for uneven ground and tricky footing. She began to brush the horse down, starting at his neck and working her way down toward his shoulder. She saw some specks of what must be mud near his left elbow and brushed over them, but they didn't flake away. She reached down, touched the biggest speck with her finger, rubbed it.

It wasn't mud. It was...

Oh, God.

She bent down, saw what looked like stippling spread across the left side of the stallion's chest, his left arm, and down to his left knee. She wasn't a forensic expert, but she'd been to her share of crime scenes. She knew what this meant.

Jack wasn't going to like it.

A moment later, he reappeared, a plastic med kit in hand. He stepped inside the stall, rested the box in the straw against one of the stall walls.

"Jack, there's something you need to see. Whoever shot Chinook—"

"Hey, boss." Chuck, a big-bellied man with ruddy cheeks, a dark mustache, and a white cowboy hat, walked in. "I looked around the corral, but I couldn't find where he was standing when he got hit. The wind has blown the snow around, and he's churned it up with his hooves. Maybe in the morning—"

"Hang on a minute." Jack held up his hand to Chuck, his gaze focused intently on Janet. "What were you about to say?"

Janet gave a slight shake of her head, tried to tell Jack without words that what she had to tell him was for his ears alone. "Nothing that can't wait."

Jack held her gaze for a moment, then looked over at Chuck. "The trouble with waiting till morning is that we're due for another foot or so of snow. Whatever is there will be buried. Get the big spotlights out and rig them up to shine down on the corral."

"Whatever you say, boss." Chuck turned and walked away.

"Spotlights?"

"We've got a rig with a couple of big halogen lights on it. We use it when we're branding calves into the night—that sort of thing. The sun doesn't always shine when we need it." He opened the box, took out a brown bottle labeled "Tea Tree Oil" and a wad of gauze. "So what were you going to tell me?"

She put her hand over the stippling on Chinook's chest. "I found—"

"I got it shoveled, boss man." The young freckle-faced man in a ski cap who'd been shoveling the sidewalk—Chuck had called him Luke—entered and approached the stall. "You need my help? I've got a lot of experience treating flesh wounds. I'm good with—"

"I can handle it. Why don't you get back to the bunkhouse, warm yourself up, get some coffee going, and then meet Chuck at the corral? It's going to be a late night."

Luke seemed to hesitate. "You want *me* to make coffee?"

The way he said it left no doubt that he felt making coffee was beneath him.

"For the love of Pete! I believe that's what I said." Jack swore under his breath. "We're all going to be cold and tired before the night's out."

Luke turned and walked away.

Janet leaned down, lowered her voice so as not to be overheard. "There's stippling on Chinook's skin—powder burns."

"Stippling?" Jack looked where she pointed, traced the pattern of dark marks with a gloved fingertip. "Son of a bitch."

"This wasn't a stray shot from some hunter's rifle. Whoever shot Chinook had to have been standing no more than a few feet away."

And Janet saw in Jack's eyes that he understood why she hadn't wanted anyone to overhear her. She saw, too, that he didn't like what she was implying.

"You think one of my men did this?"

"Who else could have gotten so close to Chinook without drawing attention to himself?"

Anger on slow burn in his chest, Jack carefully walked the length of the corral, the big halogen lamps turning night into day. "Here."

Blood on the snow.

There wasn't as much as Jack had expected, but the wind and Chinook's hooves had, indeed, taken their toll.

Chuck, Luke, and Burt came over, looked down.

Jack watched their reactions, still unable to believe one of his own men could be behind this. He'd known Chuck for decades. Burt had been with him for five years now, and though Luke was new, he'd come highly recommended and loved horses. "I can't tell for certain whether he was standing here when he was hit, or whether he simply bled into the snow here afterward."

He'd kept Janet's discovery of the stippling to himself. There was no reason to give away what they knew. But he did need to get to the bottom of it. Not only was Chinook an innocent animal in Jack's care, the stallion was also crucial to the financial well-being of the ranch, bringing in hundreds of thousands each year in stud fees and foal sales. Jack couldn't bear the thought of losing him—and neither could his bank account.

He wanted to believe it was a misfire. Maybe one of his men had been handling a pistol and had accidentally fired a shot. If so, the culprit obviously didn't have the balls to come forward and face him, knowing he'd lose his job outright.

If it had been a deliberate act …

Christ almighty.

Who would do such a thing?

He supposed it was possible that someone from that hunting party had gotten onto the property and come this close to the house. He just couldn't imagine anyone being bold or stupid enough to take that risk, especially knowing that Jack and his men were well armed. They'd have to be completely loco even to try it.

But even that unlikely scenario seemed more feasible to him than the one Janet had suggested. Why would any of his men shoot Chinook? As far as he knew, none of them harbored grudges against him. True, there'd been some grumbling when he'd put an end to smoking weed and gambling in the bunkhouse. But that had been months ago.

And yet what better way to get back at him for some misdeed, real or imagined, than to kill his beloved champion stud?

Thank God the bastard had missed! Still, Jack wanted to find the man who'd done this—and beat the shit out of him.

Chuck knelt down, touched a finger to the snow. "Why would anyone shoot a beautiful animal like Chinook?"

"I don't know." Jack had always trusted Chuck. Apart from a time or two when his foreman had been a little too free with his opinions—most particularly two years ago when those opinions involved Nate's choice of wife—Jack had never had cause even to feel irritated with the man. "Did any of the men report misfires today?"

Chuck shook his head. "I can ask around if you'd like."

"Please do. I also want to know if anyone heard anything."

"I think it's those damned hunters," Luke said.

Luke had been hired to give Nate a hand in the stables. Young and hungry to prove himself, he hadn't been here long enough for Jack to form a solid impression of him. The kid doted on Chinook and the mares.

Burt said nothing, his gaze lifting to follow Janet, who was searching the wall of the barn with a flashlight, hoping to find the bullet embedded in the wall. Burt had always been quiet, but that was fine. Jack didn't hire men to talk. Burt was a good hand with horses and cattle both and a hard worker. As far as Jack could recollect, he'd never had an occasion to complain about Burt's performance on the job—until today.

There were seventeen other men who worked and lived on the ranch, but Jack couldn't imagine any one of them doing this.

"Jack." Janet turned toward them, motioned Jack over, her stiff posture all the proof Jack needed that she was cold.

Jack stood, crossed the corral, and climbed over the fence to join her. "Find something?"

She turned the flashlight on the barn wall, where he could see a bullet hole. "Either the slug embedded here, or it went through the wall. What's on the other side?"

"A closet full of old tack and grooming gear."

She lowered her voice, her teeth chattering, her cheeks red from cold. "I wouldn't have said anything with your men standing around, but now that I've found the slug, we need to get our hands on it before the shooter does."

"You should go back inside and let me handle this. It's ten below out here, far too cold for a special agent who was fighting hypothermia earlier today, no matter how tough she thinks she is."

"I'll go back inside when you've got the slug."

"You mean to tell me you're watching my back?" It was a sweet idea, if completely absurd.

"There's no one else here I trust to do that. If the person who shot Chinook did so deliberately, there's a good chance it was done to hurt you. Since he didn't succeed in killing the stallion, he might escalate the violence and go after you directly."

"All right then." He fished his Swiss army knife out of his pocket, took Janet's flashlight, and knelt down. "It's still in here."

It was harder to dig out than he'd imagined, the wood seasoned and hard. By now, his actions had drawn the attention of his men, who stood in a group, leaning against the corral fence and watching.

"She's an FBI agent," Chuck said.

"No shit?" Burt answered. "She doesn't look like an agent."

Finally, Jack pried it loose. "Got it."

A copper-jacketed slug fell into his gloved hand.

"It's a forty-five," Janet said.

"It sure looks like it."

"You are going to bring the sheriff in on this, aren't you?"

"I haven't decided yet." Before she could object, which he could tell she was about to do, he went on. "We can talk about it—inside. I want you out of this cold now."

The storm was picking up speed, flakes falling thick and fast.

He turned to the men. "Shut the lights down and stow them away. Thanks for your help tonight, men. Warm up, and get some sleep. Chuck, lock up the stables."

Normally, they didn't lock the stables, but things weren't normal tonight. Jack would take no chances where Chinook was concerned—or Janet, for that matter.

Holding the slug in his left hand, he offered her his right arm. "It's slippery."

She tucked her arm through his, smiled. "It's okay. I won't let you fall."

CHAPTER FIVE

Sniper! Nine o'clock!

Janet jerked awake to the memory of flying bullets, sat up in bed, her body drenched in cold sweat, her heart pounding, her stomach in knots.

It was the third time tonight she'd been awakened by that same nightmare.

She turned on the light on her nightstand.

Four in the morning.

She reached for her cane, got to her feet, then went into the bathroom, where she splashed cold water on her face. She knew she ought to try to get more sleep. She was running a serious sleep deficit. But sleeping would mean dreaming, and she didn't want to dream again.

Instead, she undressed and climbed into the shower, turning the water on as hot as she could stand it, washing the dream away, letting the multiple shower heads massage tension from her back and shoulders. But as the tension began to ebb, tears came. She wasn't sure why she was crying. It was probably just stress and fatigue. Or maybe it was the nightmare. What had happened yesterday must have triggered her in some way.

Listen to yourself.

She hated how emotionally fragile she'd become. The person she'd been a year ago wouldn't have been thrown over an emotional edge by the sight of a bullet wound. It hadn't even been that serious of an injury.

Of course, she hated the fact that someone had hurt Chinook. She supposed it might have been an accident. She knew that's what Jack was hoping. People who abused animals were the worst. Lacking empathy even for innocent creatures, they were likely to hurt other people, too. She hoped Jack caught the bastard.

Oh, God, how was she going to face Jack?

Memories of last night flooded her mind, made her pulse pick up.

You're a beautiful woman.

Is that you talking—or the Côte de Brouilly?

It takes more than a few glasses of wine to make me say things I don't mean—scotch if you want poetry.

She closed her eyes, let the hot water pour over her as she remembered what his kiss had felt like—the brush of his lips against hers, the skilled teasing of his tongue, the hard feel of his body. God, she loved the way he kissed. She loved his confidence. She even loved the way he smelled.

Have you lost your mind?

Now wasn't the right time to get involved with a man. She had so far to go to get her life back together. She had finished rehab, but she was still adapting. On Monday, she was starting her new position. Most of all, she had no idea if she could even enjoy being in a relationship with a man.

Yes, she had healed, but her surgeon had cautioned her that she might find sex painful, at least for a while. He'd also warned her that pelvic damage of the kind she'd sustained often left women with some level of sexual dysfunction. She'd taken that to mean she might find it hard to

climax. She ought to have experimented on her own, tried to figure out
what still worked for her, but months of pain and narcotics and the breakup
with Byron had squelched her libido.

Still, last night had proved to her that she still had sexual needs. That
was something at least. But was she ready to go there?

No. Not yet. Her body with its new limitations and scars did not feel
like her own. She wasn't quite up to exploring its unfamiliar terrain with
another person, no matter how handsome he was.

She turned off the water, reached for a towel, dried herself, her mind
made up.

After breakfast, she would call for a tow truck and a ride back to
Denver. Her week of relaxation in the mountains was blown thanks to the
weather. While it had been kind of Jack to offer to house her for the week,
she might as well get home and face real life head-on. If she stayed, she'd
only be leading him on. Even if he had been despicably rude the first time
they'd met, he didn't deserve that.

She dried her hair, put on her makeup, and dressed, then left her room,
thinking she'd explore the library until Jack awoke. It was nearly five AM,
and with livestock to care for, he would probably be up and awake soon.

She was surprised to hear voices coming from the kitchen. She found
Jack there, drinking coffee, reading the paper, and listening to a radio
program about agricultural futures—prices on hog bellies, cattle, soybeans,
and other crops.

He looked up, smiled. "Morning. You sleep well?"

It was on the tip of her tongue to say "yes," but there was a gentleness
in his gaze that had the truth spilling out of her before she could stop it.
"No. I kept having nightmares. I finally gave up."

"Nightmares?" He frowned, got to his feet, pulled out a chair for her. "It's a good thing I've got coffee going. You take yours with milk, right?"

"You remembered." She was surprised. "How's Chinook?"

"He seems to be fine—a bit shaken up, but fine."

"Good. I'm glad to hear it. Are you going to report this to the sheriff?"

"I haven't decided."

"For what it's worth, I think you should. It costs nothing but time to file a report. The sheriff's department will be able to investigate the situation impartially. If the shooter meant to hurt you, the violence might escalate." She'd already said this, and now she would drop it.

"You're right." He poured coffee into a mug, set it down in front of her.

She needed to tell him her plans, let him know what she had in mind before he could entice her with horses or aspens or food. "I'm going to call for a tow truck today and head back to Denver."

He reached for a porcelain creamer and set it down on the table for her. "You can call for a tow truck if you'd like, but you'll have a bit of a wait. We got another eighteen inches overnight, and there was an avalanche a few miles down the canyon. I'm sorry to break the news, but the highway is closed."

She didn't like this. "How long will it take them to open it?"

"Lacking a crystal ball, I can only guess, but I'd say at least a day or two."

"Then I guess I'll stay—for a day or two."

Jack took his gaze off the icy, snow-packed highway long enough to glance over at Janet, who was bundled up and buckled into the passenger seat. He could tell she hadn't slept, dark circles beneath her eyes, her pretty face lined with fatigue.

She'd asked to come with him when he'd told her he was driving hay up to the high pasture. He'd warned her it was likely to be as exciting as watching paint dry, but she'd been all right with that. Despite his concerns about taking her along when driving conditions were almost certain to be hazardous, he was happy for the company.

"Mind if I ask what these nightmares are about?" He supposed he ought to mind his own damned business, but he didn't like the idea of her being afraid, especially not under his roof.

"It's like I'm reliving the moment I was shot. I hear Javier shout, 'Sniper! Nine o'clock!' Then gunshots ring out, and I'm down and in pain, and there's blood everywhere. I usually wake up at that point."

Combat nightmares.

Jack had had them off and on for years after coming home from Nam, and he hadn't been injured—not seriously anyway. But damned if he hadn't watched a lot of young men die, heard them screaming, seen their bodies torn apart. "Have you ever talked to anyone about your dreams?"

"Like a counselor?" She didn't look at him, her gaze focused straight ahead, her voice emotionless. "Yes. I thought they'd stopped. I haven't had them for a while. I think seeing the wound on Chinook's forearm or seeing that bullet brought it back."

"I'm sorry to hear that."

"It's not your fault."

"I invited you to enjoy the hospitality of the Cimarron, promising you a relaxing week, and I failed to deliver." This was just one more reason Jack needed to find the son of a bitch who'd pulled the trigger.

"It's not something you could have prevented."

"That's exactly why it bothers me."

He prided himself on his management of the Cimarron, on knowing what was happening from one end of his land to the other. But someone— either an outsider or an employee—had stood fifty yards from his house and shot Chinook, a prized stud who'd been born here, a horse he'd hand-raised from a colt, and Jack had no idea who had done it or why. Chuck had talked to the men, but no one had admitted to a misfire, and no one could remember seeing or hearing anything. All he had in the way of evidence was the damage to Chinook and a .45 slug.

Then another thought came to him.

"Is what happened to Chinook the reason you're in a hurry to leave— or is last night's kiss to blame?"

She looked over at him, her dark brow furrowed. "Neither. I just need to get my car in for repairs before I start my new position next week."

"I see." He did—right through her. "I came on too strong, didn't I?"

"Maybe. No. Not at all. It's just... " She hesitated. "I enjoyed kissing you, if you must know. In fact, I enjoyed it a little too much."

Back in his twenties and thirties, Jack might have thought her words were emotional nonsense, the kind of thing women said just to drive men insane. But he understood it better now—or he thought he did.

"It's about this Byron guy, isn't it? And your injuries."

She looked over at him, then quickly looked away again. "Something like that. I'm just not ready for a relationship yet."

Jack understood that, too. He'd had similar feelings. He'd gone to bed last night not only worried about Chinook, but wondering what the hell had gotten into him. He was sixty-three, a widower, a grandfather. What business did he have getting close to a woman her age? She was eighteen years younger than he was, for God's sake.

It had taken one look at her this morning to silence those doubts. She was a beautiful, desirable woman. Kissing her last night had made him feel alive again for the first time since Theresa's death. He wouldn't feel bad about that.

He reached over, took her hand. "I'm not going to rush you. There's no rushing anything up here. But please don't run off on account of me. Stay and enjoy the mountains and the horses. You've seen Chinook, but you haven't seen the mares, and you haven't ridden yet. You came up here wanting to do those things, and there's no reason you can't do them. We'll take care of the car. Don't worry."

"Where is it?"

"We passed it about a mile back."

"What?" Her head jerked around to look behind them.

"It's been completely buried, courtesy of CDOT. There's no towing company that's going to be willing to dig it out for you. My men and I will handle that when the snow lets up. In the meantime, I promise not to kiss you again. However, if you kiss me first, I *will* kiss you back. I think that's only fair, don't you?"

She looked over at him again, but this time, there was a smile on her face. "You're confident, aren't you?"

But he wasn't—not when it came to Janet.

"Here we are." He turned off the highway, lowered the plow, and began clearing a path to the pasture.

The cows were waiting for him again, lowing impatiently.

"This will take a good ten or fifteen minutes." He parked the truck. "If you start to get cold, I've got a blanket stashed behind my seat."

He got out of the truck, climbed into the back, and began cutting bales. He'd expected Janet to stay in the vehicle, but she didn't. She climbed out and walked carefully up to the fence and began having a nice chat with the cows.

"Look at you!" She reached through the fence to pet one of the animals. "You've got snow on your coat. I bet you're cold and hungry."

There was a big smile on her sweet face, fatigue and worry replaced by dimples, her dark hair catching in the cold wind. And he thought he could see just a hint of the little girl who'd read books up in apple trees.

She looked up at him, her face bright. "They're so big!"

He felt a hitch in his chest, felt his world shift on its axis.

Ah, shit!

"Wait till you see the bulls," he managed to say as he tossed hay over the fence.

After delivering hay to the cows in the high pasture, they returned to the ranch house, where Jack made an amazing breakfast of eggs, bacon, hash browns, and flapjacks, with fresh-squeezed orange juice and lots of strong coffee. Strangely, Janet didn't feel tired. When he suggested they go out and check on the horses, she felt wide awake and excited for it.

"My father started with two mares." He offered her his arm as they walked the short distance to the second of two horse barns. "He had a natural instinct for horseflesh. By the time he passed, we'd become known nationally for our quarter horses with three champion stallions. I learned from him."

He opened the door for her, let her enter first, warmth rushing over her face, the familiar scents of horses, hay, and leather welcoming her.

"Is Chinook one of yours?"

He nodded. "He was born here in these stables. He's still young as stallions go. He'll be seven in May."

"Why is he kept in a barn by himself? Doesn't that get lonely?"

"You said you had two geldings?" He said this as if it amused him, a smile tugging at his lips.

"Yes. Why?"

"Stallions can be a handful. Chinook has a strong sex drive. The moment he scents a mare in season, all he can think about is mating with her. If we put him in the same building as the mares, he would tear the place apart. He'd wreak havoc every time one of them was in estrus. He'd kick down his stall, tear down hers, and attack any horse—mare or gelding—that got in his way. As for being lonely, he gets a lot of female attention during the breeding season, and we keep him busy."

She'd had no idea stallions could be that difficult to handle. "So you just bring the mares to him when it's time?"

"More or less."

"How many mares does he breed each season?"

"He sires probably a hundred-twenty foals each year."

"Good grief! He must be very proud of himself." But that raised another question. "How do you know when the mares are fertile?"

"Some stallions have good enough manners that you can use them to tease the mares and gauge where they are in their cycles, but not Chinook.

We use ultrasounds and palpation to check the mares, and then bring them to him when they're in deep estrus."

"It sounds like quite an operation."

They turned a corner, and Janet had to fight not to squeal. A dozen stalls stretched out before her, each one holding a beautiful palomino quarter horse, their coats ranging from the almost silver color of Chinook's to deep golden and even chocolate hues. Their heads came up, and there was a ripple of excitement as they recognized Jack.

Janet walked up to the first stall. "Hi, beautiful."

The mare tossed her head and walked over to greet Jack, who took a carrot out of his coat pocket and handed it to Janet. "That's Baby Doe. Last time we bred her, she ended up pregnant with twins and had a partial uterine torsion. We had to ship her off to Colorado State University for round-the-clock care. We got lucky. She survived, and so did both of the foals—a rare thing with twins."

"I'm so glad she's okay." Janet held the carrot out on her palm, felt the mare's lips brush softly over her hand as she took the carrot and began to crunch. "I thought I knew a lot about horses, but in the past five minutes, I've discovered that I really don't. And thanks for the carrot."

Jack grinned. "I wanted you to make a good first impression."

She moved to the next stall, where a pale mare was craning her neck, trying to get at some stray hay. Using her cane to help her balance, Janet bent carefully down and picked up the hay, then held it out on her palm. "Who's this?"

"This is Molly Brown."

Janet saw a pattern. "You've named the mares after famous Colorado women."

Jack grinned. "Seemed like a good thing to do."

"I like it."

In short order, she'd fed carrots to Chipeta, Isabella Bird, Julia Greeley, and a sweet little yearling filly named Clara Brown.

Then they came to an enormous gelding. "He's huge!"

"That's Buckwheat, my granddaughter's horse. He's the first horse Emily rode, and she fell in love with him."

"I can see why." Janet stroked the velvet of his muzzle.

"He's a big old softie, aren't you, Buckwheat?"

The gelding whickered, nuzzled Jack, who patted his shoulder. "I thought we'd tack him up, get you up on his back, and let you get a feel for riding again—if you're up to it, that is."

Janet gaped at him, her heart ricocheting around inside her ribcage. "I don't know. How will I mount him? What if I fall?"

"We had a veteran who was a triple amputee ride Buckwheat last summer. I once watched a woman who was paralyzed from the waist down ride him. You'll do fine."

Up until this moment, riding had been an abstract thought, a wish, not a real plan. Now that she was faced with getting up on a horse again, she couldn't tell if her heart was pounding from excitement or fear. But if amputees and people who were paralyzed had the courage to try, then, damn it, so did she.

"Okay. Let's do this."

"You've got it." Jack grinned, entered Buckwheat's stall, clipped a lead rope to the gelding's halter, and led him out of the stall and down the center walkway to a hallway, the walls of which were hung with tack. He tied off Buckwheat's lead rope and began to saddle him. "You're ready for some exercise, aren't you, boy?"

She watched while Jack saddled and bridled Buckwheat, some part of her unable to believe she was really going to do this.

"We'll have you mount him from the left side using our larger mounting block so that I can be there to support you," Jack was saying.

Janet only heard part of that, her mouth dry. "Okay."

He checked the girth, then took hold of Buckwheat's reins. "Come on, buddy."

Janet followed them around a corner and down a short hallway to a sliding door that opened to reveal the attached riding barn—an enormous structure with a floor of groomed sand. It was chilly compared to the barn, but she barely noticed the cold, the idea that she was about to mount a horse driving all other thoughts away.

Jack led Buckwheat a few feet inside the riding barn, then waited for her to catch up. "Mind holding the reins? I need to get the mounting block."

Janet took the reins, stroked Buckwheat's powerful neck, spoke in soothing tones to the gelding, though it was her own nerves she was trying to quell. "We're going to get along just fine, aren't we?"

Jack returned in less than a minute, carrying a large mounting block. It had three steps and space on top that was big enough to accommodate two people. He set it down on Buckwheat's left side, then checked the tightness of the girth once again. He reached for the reins. "Ms. Killeen, your steed awaits."

Janet took a deep breath, started up the steps, Jack's strong hand on her waist as he followed her. She reached the top, turned to face the horse, instinctively reaching for the saddle horn, her cane still in her right hand. "How do I do this?"

"Take hold of the saddle, lean into me, and lift your left foot into the stirrup."

She tried to do what he'd suggested, but she had trouble controlling her left foot to get it into the stirrup. She just couldn't make it flex. But before she could give up, he knelt down, caught her foot, and guided it into position.

"Lean on me, and swing your right leg over."

Janet was about to lift her right leg, when Buckwheat shifted. She lost her balance, her pulse rocketing. "Shit!"

Strong arms held her fast. "I've got you."

She looked into Jack's eyes, tears pricking her eyes. "I'm afraid."

"I know you are, but you can do this. I know you can. Try again, and don't let his movements spook you. He's not going anywhere, and neither am I."

"Will you ride with me? Maybe if you're on the horse, too… "

He nodded. "Sure. But you're mounting first. You need to do this so that you know you can."

"Okay." Janet dropped her cane behind her, letting it fall into the sand. She took hold of the saddle horn with her left hand, and put her weight on her left foot, leaning into Jack for support as she lifted her right leg over the gelding's back.

And then she was sitting in the saddle.

"I did it!" She buried her fingers in the gelding's thick, blond mane.

"Yes, you did." Jack swung up into the saddle behind her, wrapped one arm around her waist, his thighs pressed against hers, his chest hard against her back. "Are you in any pain?"

He was so close that she could feel his breath against her hair, his voice deep, his scent surrounding her.

She shook her head, not wanting to tell him exactly what she was feeling at this particular moment. "I'm fine."

"That's what I wanted to hear." Holding the reins in his left hand, he urged Buckwheat forward. "Come on, boy. The lady wants to ride."

CHAPTER SIX

Jack walked Buckwheat around the barn, giving the gelding time to get used to their weight and Janet time to adjust to sitting in the saddle. "How does it feel?"

"It feels great."

He glanced down, saw the dimple in her cheek, and knew she was smiling.

There was something healing about horses. He had watched his son help Megan, who'd suffered terrible sexual abuse and misuse as a teen, learn to trust again by riding in this very barn. He'd watched friends of Nate's, veterans who'd been burned and maimed, rediscover a sense of masculinity through riding. He'd watched dozens of children—autistic kids, kids from abusive homes, kids with terminal illnesses—find joy through the equine therapy program to which the Cimarron donated horses.

He hoped Janet would find healing here, too, though not purely for unselfish reasons. If she enjoyed herself during her stay, maybe she'd come back, and maybe…

You're getting ahead of yourself, old man.

"Ready to go faster?"

"Yes!"

Jack decided not to trot the horse, given that it would make Janet bounce in the saddle, something that could be uncomfortable and tiring even for riders without injuries. Instead, he brought Buckwheat to a lope.

In front of him, Janet laughed, the sound like music. "This is wonderful!"

"I'm glad you're enjoying it."

It stirred his blood being close to her like this, her bottom touching his thighs, her back pressed against his chest, her sweet scent filling his head. He was as aware of her as he was the big animal that moved beneath them, and could feel that she was aware of him, too. He tightened his thighs around the horse and felt her tense. He adjusted his hold around her waist and heard her quick inhalation. He rested his cheek against the silk of her hair and felt her relax into him.

If they'd had decent weather, he would have been able to take her on a ride around the ranch. He would have packed a lunch and a bottle of wine and taken her up on one of the trails that passed through groves of old-growth aspens. But the snow was too deep, and he wouldn't want her out there now anyway, not until he knew who'd shot Chinook and why. And so they were confined to the barn.

Janet didn't seem to mind, and neither did Buckwheat, who tugged at the bit, wanting to let loose.

"Think you can handle a gallop?"

"Bring it on!"

Jack let the gelding have his head, and off they went, galloping in circles and figure-eights, Janet's laughter making him smile. She showed no fear, but sat a horse well, her body's response to the animal's motions instinctive and fluid. He'd have been able to tell she was an experienced rider even if she hadn't told him.

When he sensed that Buckwheat's restless energy was spent, he brought him to a lope and then back to a walk.

"How did that feel?"

"Wonderful." Her voice was tight, a single tear trickling down her cheek.

It must be hell to have one's life torn apart like she had. Yes, Jack had endured his share of loss, but he'd never been the one to suffer. He'd seen his fellow Rangers die in combat. He'd found his wife's lifeless body. He'd had to watch while Nate dealt with the unimaginable pain and suffering of his burns, then had his own heart broken as his son came to grips with living life with a disfigured face. But Jack's life had changed very little, revolving around the ranch and the changing seasons as it always had.

Janet hadn't been as badly wounded as Nate, but the life she'd known was gone just the same. It felt good to be able to give some part of that life back to her.

Jack walked Buckwheat, let the gelding cool down, and then brought him to a halt back at the mounting block. Jack dismounted first, then helped Janet. He let her do most of the work, but kept one arm around her waist just in case. She felt slender and soft in his arms, every inch a woman.

As her left foot came out of the stirrup, she lost her balance. "Oh!"

"I've got you." He caught her, held her fast.

For a moment they stood face to face, his arms around her, their bodies pressed together, her palms flat against his chest.

She smiled, a trail of moisture on each cheek from her tears. "Thank you."

"You're welcome." He wiped her tears away with the pads of his thumbs, his gaze dropping to her mouth. Her lips tempted him. Hell, yes, they did.

But he'd made a promise, and he'd keep that promise until hell froze over and he'd walked five miles on the ice.

Still holding fast to Buckwheat's reins, he turned and helped her down the stairs. "I just want to point out that you got down without your cane."

She looked up at him, surprise in those green eyes. "I completely forgot about it. Well, I had your help."

Jack walked over and retrieved it from the sand. "Here you go."

"Thank you." She took it from him, smiled. "By the way, I've decided to stay the week—if that's still okay."

"I've been waiting for you to say that."

It only bothered him a little to think she was most likely staying for the horses and not because of him.

Janet followed Jack back to the stables, her pulse still pounding from the thrill of their ride, her heart lighter than it had been in months. She'd actually sat in the saddle and ridden again—thanks to Jack. She wasn't certain she'd have done it if he hadn't been there to push and help her.

He'd called himself an "old codger" yesterday, but that's not what she saw when she looked at him. She saw a man who was gentle with both animals and people. She saw a man who loved the land, did strenuous work in the outdoors, and lived according to his own creed. The fact that he was incredibly good looking, physically fit, and kissed like a god only made him more amazing.

Riding together, his arm around her waist, the hard wall of his chest behind her, had left her feeling more aware of herself as a woman than she'd felt in a very long time. When they'd stood together on the mounting block moments ago, she'd seen his gaze drop to her mouth and had found herself fighting the urge to kiss him. It would have been so easy, and she would have loved every moment of it. But she didn't want to start something she couldn't finish. It wouldn't be fair to him.

Jack was telling her about the stables—when they'd been built and rebuilt, something about a fire—but his words barely registered, her attention fixed on the way he walked, the innate grace of his stride, his skill with the horse and, yes, okay, his ass. She could hardly blame herself. He *did* look fantastic in a pair of well-worn jeans.

She watched as Jack clipped cross ties to the bridle, removed first the saddle and then the saddle blanket, hanging them from hooks on the wall. She found a curry comb and began to rub the gelding down, starting at his neck. "Was Buckwheat born here, too?"

"Yeah, he was. Chipeta is his dam. He was sired by a stallion from another ranch. He had some conformation flaws, particularly around his head, so we gelded him just after he was weaned. He's a damned good cattle horse and has a great disposition."

Janet glanced up, her gaze drawn again to Jack, who had grabbed another comb and was working on Buckwheat's other side. "What qualities do you look for when you decide which colts get to keep their balls?"

Jack met her gaze over Buckwheat's back, one dark eyebrow arching, a grin tugging at his lips. "A good mind and disposition—those are the most important. After that, I look for correct conformation—straight legs, good hips and shoulders, a nice head and neck. A colt that doesn't meet all of those criteria gets gelded. There are other things that can tip the scale—

gait, athletic ability. What I'm looking for is a perfect representation of the breed."

"How often do you find that?"

"I'd say one out of fifteen to twenty foals makes the cut."

She winced at his choice of words. "Or escapes it."

Jack grinned. "We do use anesthesia, you know. It's not like I chase them around the corral with a machete. Besides, geldings live much more contented lives than stallions."

"How do you figure? Chinook has more sex than most people, while poor Buckwheat here gets nothing."

"Stallions are slaves to their biology. Their lives carry a fair amount of stress. They're biologically geared to do two things: fight and mate."

"That sounds like a lot of the guys I've helped put in the penitentiary."

He chuckled. "There are times I've wondered if we wouldn't make the world a better place by treating human males more like we treat colts."

"So now we're talking about mating people?" The words were out before she could stop them. Was she flirting with him?

"Well, I was talking more about castrating some of the male variety, but if your mind is on mating, that's okay. Let's go there."

"What qualities would you look for in a woman?"

She *was* flirting with him—and he was flirting back.

He laughed. "If I had the mindset of a stallion, only one—willingness. For a male of any species, success at mating is all about spreading your seed."

"That's lovely." That also described a lot of the men she'd known.

"Fortunately, I am not ruled by biology. It's brains over balls."

"Meaning what?" She looked up, her gaze connecting with his.

"Meaning I spent thirty-eight years making a study of just one woman, trying to be the man she deserved."

In his words, Janet heard the love he'd felt for his wife. He'd been devoted to her, and he'd been faithful to her. Then he'd lost her.

She realized she was staring at him, her hand motionless on the gelding's flank. "You must miss her very much."

"I do." Jack smiled, his blue eyes looking into hers. "But lately I've been thinking life just might have a few surprises left for me."

And Janet found it hard to breathe.

Jack fixed cross ties to Chinook's halter then held fast to the cheek piece to steady the animal, knowing full well that ropes wouldn't hold the stallion if he were truly frightened or upset. "No sudden sounds or movements, and we'll be fine. If your camera has a flash on it, turn it off."

Det. Sgt. Taylor, a young man perhaps in his thirties, made an adjustment to his camera, then moved closer to photograph the wound on the stallion's forearm and the stippling on his skin, the camera's electronic buzz making Chinook nervous.

Jack hadn't wanted to get outsiders involved in his problems, but Janet had made him realize that he really had no choice, not if he wanted to protect his horses and find the shooter.

When Taylor was done, Sheriff Rove bent down to examine the wound. "Sure looks like a graze to me. You say you found the slug?"

Jack reached into his coat pocket and drew out the plastic sandwich bag that held the slug. "Ms. Killeen found it embedded in the barn wall. I'll take you outside and show you where she found it when you're finished here."

The sheriff took the bag, looked at the slug. "It's a forty-five for sure. You're the one who found it, ma'am?"

Janet stood at a respectful distance beside Chuck. "Yes."

Because she'd been here when the shooting had happened, Janet would probably be asked to make a statement. Jack hated seeing her get dragged into this. He didn't want her having nightmares again.

The sheriff was still examining the slug, a frown on his face. "I had some hunters report a forty-five stolen from one of their vehicles a couple of days before the storm hit—a Kimber 1911 with custom camo grips. They admitted to trespassing on your land and said they thought you had taken it to get back at them."

"Is that so? Why is this the first I've heard about it?"

Sheriff Rove handed the plastic bag with the slug over to his detective. "I didn't want to bother you. I figured it was bullshit."

"It *is* bullshit." Jack had never stolen anything from anyone. "We had contact with a party of hunters a few days before the storm broke. I asked them to leave my land, but I sure as hell didn't take a firearm from them."

Then Janet spoke up. "Could they have planned this? Maybe they reported the weapon stolen, then used it to shoot Chinook to get back at you. That way, there'd be a record of the pistol being stolen if it were ever found. They'd be off the hook."

That was an interesting thought.

The sheriff shot Jack an amused look. "Just because the gun that was stolen was a forty-five and this slug is a forty-five doesn't mean the two are connected in any way. Forty-five handguns are very common, ma'am."

Jack didn't like Rove's response. True, Rove was an old dog, but that was no excuse for dismissing a woman's opinion out of hand, especially when that woman was a hell of a lot smarter than he was. "Ms. Killeen is an FBI special agent."

Rove's eyes widened almost imperceptibly. "It's a good theory, I guess, but that's giving these fellows entirely too much credit. I doubt they can chew gum and tie their boots at the same time, much less come up with a plan like that. Besides, they cleared off the day before the storm, headed back to Denver. They wanted to catch a flight home before the snow started flying."

But Janet had gotten Jack thinking. *He* hadn't taken the weapon, but that didn't mean one of his men hadn't. What better way to commit a crime than to do it with a weapon that couldn't be tied to you?

Of course, Sheriff Rove was right. The fact that both weapons had been forty-fives could easily be a coincidence. Up here, everyone owned at least one.

The detective put away his camera. "With your permission, Mr. West, I'd like to interview everyone who was on the property the day your stallion was shot—family, friends, employees."

Jack had expected as much. "I'll provide you with a list of our personnel and arrange for you to speak privately with each one of them in my office."

He hoped Taylor had better luck finding answers than Chuck had.

"Thank you."

"Boy, I tell you, it sure is a mystery." The sheriff shoved both of his hands in his pockets, which was probably where he kept them most of the time.

"It can't be that big of a mystery," Janet said. "Either it was an accident, or it was deliberate. If it was deliberate, then we need to look for motive. Bullets are fired from weapons held by people who have some reason for pulling the trigger. It's not like this bullet came from outer space."

Sheriff Rove's round cheeks turned red, and he immediately tried to cover his ass. "What I meant was that it's a mystery as to why anyone would want to harm such a fine animal. Normally, we send animal control to respond to these kinds of calls, but I take a special interest in what happens at the Cimarron."

Maybe it was time for Jack to take a special interest in county elections and see that they got some new blood in the sheriff's office.

"Chuck, will you see Ms. Killeen safely back to the house?" Jack turned to Taylor. "If you'll give me a moment to get Chinook back into his stall, I'll walk the sheriff to his car and then see you get what you need."

Janet opened her eyes, glanced around. When had she fallen asleep? Someone had draped a throw blanket over her and set the book she'd been reading—a biography of John Adams—on the end table, her page bookmarked. That same someone had also started a fire in the fireplace.

How kind he was, how thoughtful. With a few simple gestures, he made her feel cared for, pampered, special. Byron on his best day couldn't have managed that.

Outside the floor-to-ceiling windows, the sun had already set, snowflakes drifting lazily from sky to ground. She'd been asleep for a while.

She'd given her statement to Taylor and then come here to occupy herself while Jack dealt with his men. It had taken most of the afternoon.

She pushed aside the blanket, reached for her cane, and got to her feet, her hip stiff, the muscles of her inner thighs sore from today's ride. It had been a long time since she'd been saddle sore. She made her way out into the hallway, where she heard music coming from the gym—Led Zeppelin's "Black Dog."

She walked down the hall and found the door open. Wearing a black Army Ranger tank and black gym shorts, Jack stood at a cable machine doing standing cable flyes. He didn't seem to notice her, but worked his way through the set, exhaling each time he drew his hands together in front of his chest, the muscles of his arms and shoulders taut.

Now she knew why his body felt so hard and muscular.

He finished the last set, released the cables, and played a few chords of air guitar before reaching for his stainless steel water bottle.

Not wanting to startle him—or get caught staring—she knocked on the door jamb.

His head jerked around. He smiled when he saw her.

Her stomach did a flip.

"Hey. Did you have a nice nap?"

"Yes, thank you." She walked over to him, the sheen of sweat on his forehead somehow sexy. "Thanks for the blanket—and the fire. I was snug and cozy. Did everything work out with the detective?"

He frowned. "That depends on how you look at it. He took statements from everyone, but none of them saw or heard anything. I've got twenty men out there, and not one of them noticed when someone aimed a gun at the ranch's prized stallion?"

"I'm sorry. It must be incredibly upsetting."

"I thought I'd burn off some frustration and take a shower before making dinner."

"Don't let me bother you."

"Why don't you join me?"

She blinked. "You're serious?"

He was. "You can work in between my sets."

There was no reason she couldn't. She hadn't lifted weights since being shot, but that was only because she'd had to devote all her time and energy to physical therapy.

"Okay. I'll be right back." She hurried to her room, changed into a pair of yoga pants, a sports bra, and an old T-shirt, then pulled her hair back into a loose ponytail.

In less than ten minutes, she was back in the gym, where Brett Eldredge was singing "Beat of the Music." So Jack wasn't just a classic rock guy.

"What kind of workout do you usually do?"

"I haven't done anything since I was shot. I just had too much else going on." She figured he needed to know that. "I used to aim for three days a week on weights—one day for chest, shoulders, and triceps, one for back, abs and biceps, and one for glutes, hamstrings, quads, and calves."

He nodded. "I'm doing chest and shoulders today, so why don't we start there?"

They took turns doing chest press, triceps press, and more cable flyes, Jack adjusting the weight, spotting for Janet, and encouraging her. She tried not to stare at him while he lifted, then gave up, the sight of all that man and shifting muscle more than she was able or willing to deny herself. As they moved from one set to the next, she grew more and more aroused until she was certifiably horny.

She hadn't felt like this in ages.

At first, they talked about the sheriff's visit. The guy was an idiot as far as Janet could tell, and she told Jack so. "I don't think he plans on doing anything."

"Neither do I."

"Who went with you when you confronted the hunters?" The frown on his face told her that he knew where she was headed with that question.

"You think one of them might have taken it."

"I know you don't want to doubt your men, but I find it highly unlikely that some stranger walked out of a blizzard, shot Chinook without being seen, then disappeared into the storm." She could see in his eyes that it hurt him even to consider that one of his men might have betrayed him.

He had such expressive eyes.

"I understand what you're saying. If one of them planned to get back at me, it might make sense for him to acquire a firearm that couldn't be traced to him."

"It might be a total coincidence that both weapons are forty-fives."

"Then again, it might not." He stopped to take a drink of water. "I already had Chuck make up a list of the dozen men who went with me. I faxed it to the detective this afternoon."

So he'd already been thinking along those lines.

Smart man.

The conversation drifted from the shooting to working out and then to music. By the time they were finished, she was sweaty, and her arms felt like linguine, endorphins humming through her veins, where they collided with a healthy dose of pheromones.

"That's the second thing you've done today that you haven't done in a while. How did it feel?" He turned off the iPod, the room going silent.

"It felt terrific." She wanted so badly to kiss him.

No, kissing wouldn't be enough. She wanted to rip his clothes off and make good use of the weight bench. Then she remembered why she couldn't have sex with him, or why it would be very awkward and possibly mortifyingly embarrassing if she tried, and her good mood plummeted.

"I should shower," she said.

Then she turned and walked back to her room.

CHAPTER SEVEN

Jack showered and dressed, then called Nate to give him an update. "Are you sure you don't want me to come home? They've reopened the highway. Megan and Emily can last a few days here without me. She's got her brother and his posse nearby if she needs anything."

"No, son, there's no need for you to head up the canyon. Sheriff Rove seems to have it all in hand."

"Sheriff Rove is an idiot, and you know it. That man is so fat and lazy he probably hasn't seen his own dick in twenty years."

That was true enough.

"His detective sergeant, a young man by the name of Taylor, seems to know what he's doing. He came and photographed the whole thing and interviewed all the men yesterday."

"I think I should be there."

Jack hadn't wanted to come out with this, but he could see he didn't have a choice. "Truth is, son, I've got company, and the privacy has been good."

A long pause.

"Are you entertaining a lady friend, old man?"

Nate had never been stupid.

"As a matter of fact, I am. Do you remember Janet Killeen?"

"Isn't she that pretty FBI agent you tossed off the property last winter?"

Had it really been that bad?

"She was on her way up to the Forest Creek Inn in Scarlet when she went off the road about a mile from the turnoff to the high pasture. She spent almost twenty-four hours in her car. CDOT had all but buried it by the time I found her. I brought her here, and we're having a good time."

"I see." The tone of Nate's voice left no doubt as to what exactly he thought Jack meant by "good time."

"Not *that* kind of good time." Not yet, anyway, but Jack wasn't in a hurry.

"She was badly wounded, wasn't she? I heard she might not walk again."

"She is walking, though she uses a cane. Being here with the horses has been good for her." He didn't share with Nate the fact that Janet was suffering from nightmares. That was her personal business.

"It's just the *horses* that are good for her?"

Smart ass.

"She grew up on a farm, and today we got her up on Buckwheat. It was the first time she'd ridden since being shot. She's a good rider and has a natural touch with horses, even Chinook."

"I'm happy to hear that." Nate truly did sound pleased.

"I'm glad I have your approval." Jack meant it as a joke, but he truly did feel relief at his son's reaction.

Nate and his mother had been very close. It was one thing for Nate to encourage him to date. It was something else for Nate to feel comfortable with Jack bringing a woman into their home.

"What I don't like is some shooter walking around on our land while you're busy with the lovely Ms. Killeen."

"We're keeping the horses indoors and exercising them in the riding barn. I'm not taking any chances."

"How's Luke working out?"

"He is rising to the challenge. He seems very eager to prove his worth."

"A bit too eager sometimes. It can be annoying."

Jack laughed. "He'll get the hang of things soon enough. I'm having a video surveillance system installed in the barns next Monday. In the meantime, he and Chuck are taking turns sleeping outside Chinook's stall."

"A video surveillance system? That will be expensive."

"Losing Chinook would be a lot more expensive."

"True enough."

"I need to get to the kitchen. The biscuits won't make themselves."

"Before you go, I have some news."

"Yeah?"

"Megan's pregnant." Nate didn't sound happy about it.

Jack found himself smiling, but he bit back his congratulations. He knew the two of them had agreed to wait until after Megan finished law school. She was only halfway through her first semester. "I take it this came as a surprise. When did you get the news?"

"This morning. We haven't told Emily yet."

"How does Megan feel about it?"

"She's excited but worried about how pregnancy and a new baby will affect her ability to get through law school."

"Understandable. You can reassure her, of course, that we will do all we can to make sure she gets the support she needs."

"This is my fault."

Jack chuckled. "Now, son, I thought we had that talk. You knew going into this how it all works."

"She forgot to take a couple pills, and she warned me. I thought there was no way a couple of pills could make a difference, so I didn't take extra precautions."

"Well, there's only one thing to say now. Congratulations. I'll admit it. I'm excited. A new baby in the house? That's great."

Children brought chaos, but Jack did all right with chaos. He loved being a grandfather as much as he'd loved being a father, except that he was wiser now, more patient. He probably made a better grandpa than he had a dad.

"Thanks. I appreciate the support. Keep me posted on the situation with Chinook."

"I will. Pass my congratulations and love to Megan, and give Miss Emily a hug. We can celebrate your news when you get home next weekend."

"Thanks, Dad."

Jack ended the call, then got to work in the kitchen mixing up a batch of buttermilk biscuits, a big smile on his face. He'd just pulled them from the oven when Janet appeared, freshly showered, her hair glossy from having been blown dry.

She'd put on a bit of makeup—just enough to highlight her beautiful eyes—and a lavender turtleneck with a pair of Levis. Damned if she didn't fill out both the shirt and her jeans to perfection.

She smiled. "It smells delicious."

"The stew was made with beef raised here on the ranch. I tossed in potatoes, carrots, onions, green beans, and my own special ingredient—hard cider brewed in Scarlet Springs."

"If I lived here, I'd get fat." Janet took the basket of rolls from him and set it on the table, then found the butter crock and did the same with it.

"If you lived here, I'd keep you too busy for you to get fat."

"Is that so?"

"You better believe it."

Only when Jack saw the blush in Janet's cheeks did he realize how she'd taken his words. He'd been thinking of her working with the horses. He wondered for a moment whether he should correct her impression, then decided against it. He didn't want to embarrass her or hurt her feelings, and if her mind had immediately gone to sex, he was okay with that.

He served the stew and the salad, then got two bottles of hard cider out of the fridge, poured them into mugs, and set one at each plate. "Help yourself."

"Tell me about Nate and Megan and your granddaughter—Emily is her name?"

Jack told her about the news he'd just gotten, then bragged about Nate's accomplishments and how proud he'd been when Nate had made the cut to serve as a special operator with a Marines special ops team that worked with Navy SEALs.

"That's how he met Javier Corbray, isn't it?"

"Yes, it is." Jack told her how Nate had courageously faced his burns, how hard he'd fought to live. Then he told her how Nate had met Megan when she'd been volunteering at one of the homeless shelters to which the Cimarron donated ground beef. He told her how Megan hadn't been repulsed by Nate's scars, but had helped him accept himself and heal. "I thank God every day for Megan."

"She sounds like a special person."

"That she is. Emily was Megan's daughter by a previous relationship. The man is dead, and we don't talk about him. Nate adopted Emily when he and Megan got married."

Jack didn't tell her about Megan's scars—her long battle with heroin addiction, her time in prison, the sexual abuse she'd suffered there, the baby daddy who'd terrorized her. He also didn't mention the fact that Nate had been the one to kill Emily's biological father, saving both mother and daughter. Megan's past was hers to share if and when she felt comfortable doing so.

If Janet stuck around, she would eventually get the whole story. If she didn't, she had no need to know.

"I love happy endings." Janet dabbed her lips with her napkin. "I bet Emily has you wrapped around her little finger."

"I wouldn't say that." That was a bald-faced lie, and Jack knew it. "Okay, yes, she does. What can I say? I love that kid."

"You're a very nurturing man."

"Thank you." He knew some men wouldn't like being described that way. Hell, it might have rubbed him the wrong way thirty years ago. But now, he appreciated it. "I wasn't always. I married a woman, then signed up to fight in a war on the other side of the world, leaving her with my parents. But I've learned a thing or two since then."

Janet took a sip of her cider, smiled. "I bet you have."

And damned if it wasn't his turn to blush.

Janet searched through the Cimarron's library of DVDs and Blu-Rays. Jack had left it up to her to pick the movie. She didn't think she could handle anything with violence. Detective dramas and procedurals made her feel like she was at work, when their inaccuracies and Hollywoodisms didn't drive her crazy.

"Oh!" She took *The Sound of Music* off the shelf. "I haven't seen this in ages. Is it too much of a kids' movie for you?"

Jack, who was finishing making popcorn at the little bar at the back of the theater room, glanced up. "That's fine with me."

She carried the DVD over to him.

He handed her a big bowl of popcorn. "Go pick a seat."

She sat in the center of the theater's front row, the bowl of popcorn on her lap, the buttery scent of the corn making her mouth water. How she could possibly have room for this after Jack's delicious stew, she couldn't say.

He came and sat beside her. "Have you figured out how to work the seats?"

"I guess not." She wasn't even sure what he meant.

He reached across her, pushed a button on the arm of her chair. Her seat began to recline, and a footrest came up.

"Wow. This is better than a real theater."

"Damned straight." He raised a remote, and the lights dimmed.

Janet lost herself in the film, forgetting the real world, aware only of the story taking shape on the screen and the man beside her. She glanced over at him, the rugged features of his face softened by the blue light from the screen.

She must be crazy even thinking of starting a relationship with him. Then again, what was crazy about it? They were both unattached. They both had successful careers. Despite her first impression of him, he was a good man, not the kind who'd bolt when life got hard. He was tough, but there was a gentleness inside him she'd rarely seen in a man. He'd been faithful to his wife. He'd stood by his critically injured son. And because he was already a father and grandfather, he wouldn't care that she couldn't have kids. She hadn't had a period in months, after all.

Of course, she would have to tell him everything. Before things went too far, she would have to tell him that she might not be able to have sex with him, at least not in the usual way. It was that thought more than anything that held her back.

No, it was the fear of finding out the truth, of trying to be close with a man, only to discover that it hurt or that she couldn't come. She'd always loved sex, loved getting close with a man, body and soul. The possibility that she *might* not be able to enjoy sex was far easier to live with than the certainty that she definitely could not.

Up on the screen, kids dressed in repurposed drapes were running all over Salzburg singing "Do-Re-Mi."

She glanced over at Jack again, felt a tug in her chest. "By the way, you can put your arm around my shoulders if you'd like."

"I would like." Jack raised the armrest that divided their two seats, reached over, and drew her closer.

She rested her head against his chest, heard the steady beating of his heart, and felt her blood warm as his fingers caressed her shoulder. She was contemplating the wisdom of turning in her seat and kissing him when his cell phone rang.

"Sorry." He drew it out of his pocket, glanced down. "It's Chuck."

Janet got a bad feeling.

Jack answered. "What's up?"

His body went tense. He withdrew his arm and pushed the button to bring his seat upright. "Is he okay? Have you called for an ambulance or the sheriff? I'm on my way."

"What is it?" Janet fumbled for the button on her seat.

He raised the remote control, brought the lights up, and stopped the movie. "An intruder entered the stallion's barn. Luke has been shot."

"Oh, my God." She'd been afraid something like this would happen.

Jack looked furious. "It's not serious. Luke fired back, but whoever it was has run off. Chinook wasn't hurt, but he's gone berserk and is kicking the hell out of his stall."

She reached for her cane, got to her feet. "What can I do to help?"

"Stay inside and out of danger." He started to move around her.

She blocked his path. "I'm not letting you go out there alone."

He cupped her face in his hands, and his gaze softened. "An armed man is loose on my land somewhere, and I don't want you coming into the line of fire. My men and I can handle it."

She stepped back, glared up at him. "I'm better trained than most of your men. Give me a weapon."

He frowned, a muscle clenching in his jaw. "All right, but you stick with me. I'm *not* putting a firearm in your hands, not because I don't trust you, but because you haven't fired one since the day you were shot. Your having a gun won't help any of us if you're not ready to use it."

His words stung, but she knew what he said was true. "Fair enough."

"I'll meet you in the mudroom." He walked out of the theater and headed down the hallway toward his office.

She hurried to the mudroom, picking up a notepad and pen from the kitchen counter along the way. By the time she had her boots on, he was there, looking grim-faced, a Colt M1911 in a shoulder holster. He put on his boots, grabbed a barn jacket. "Someone just bought himself a world of trouble."

"He sure has." She followed Jack outside, took his arm when he offered it. She could hear the stallion's frenzied whinnies and wished she could run, because surely that's what Jack wanted to do. "He must be terrified. You should go on without me."

"I'm *not* leaving you out here in the dark by yourself with a gunman around."

This is why he'd wanted her to stay in the house. He'd known this would happen, and yet he still refused to leave her without protection.

"Sorry. I'm slowing you down. I'm just not used to sitting on the sidelines."

"I know. We're almost there."

Inside the stables, they found chaos. Chuck stood outside Chinook's stall trying to calm him, but the stallion bucked, reared, and lunged, his hooves chipping wood, denting the walls of his stall, his teeth bared. Luke sat shirtless on a cot, Burt pressing gauze to his shoulder with gloved hands. A half dozen of the other men stood around watching, some of them holding firearms.

Janet lowered her voice to a whisper. "This is a crime scene. We need to get everyone out of here and lock it down."

"We certainly do." Jack walked over to the men who were milling about. "There's nothing you can do here, men. Head back to the bunkhouse, and get some sleep. The sheriff's investigators will probably have some questions for you later. If we need your help in the meantime, we'll let you know."

The respect the men had for Jack was evident. He projected a calm that seemed to settle everyone. Janet knew that quality for what it was—leadership.

"You got it, boss."

"We'll find this son of a bitch."

"We're here for you, Mr. West."

Jack walked over to Luke. "Burt, why don't you walk Luke up to the house and get ready to take him to the hospital in Scarlet?"

"It was Kip, boss." Luke looked like he was fighting not to cry. "I guess he came to finish what he started, but I stopped him."

There was stippling on Luke's face and chest.

"Who's Kip?" Janet went to stand beside Luke.

"He's a guy who got himself fired a few weeks back," Burt said.

A disgruntled employee. A man with a possible motive.

"Can you tell me what happened?" Janet asked.

Luke was shaking now, the aftermath of adrenaline. "I was sleeping, when I heard the door. I looked up and saw a man standing just inside the barn. I asked who he was and what he was doing. He walked closer, said his name was Kip. I could see he was holding a gun. I reached for my pistol, and he shot me. I fired back, but I guess I missed. He took off running."

Janet wrote all of this down. "Where was he standing when he fired his weapon?"

Luke pointed to near where she was standing. "He came up on me pretty close."

The powder burns on Luke's face and chest seemed to corroborate that.

"How many shots did he fire?"

"Just the one."

"How many shots did you fire?"

"One, I think. Maybe two."

Jack rested a hand on Luke's uninjured shoulder. "Let's get you fixed up first, and then we'll talk about what happened at the hospital."

Janet knew Jack was right. If she'd been here in an official capacity, her first duty would be to make sure that anyone who was wounded received medical care. Statements could wait. As it was, she was here as a guest, not an agent.

Jack gave her arm a reassuring squeeze, demonstrating his understanding and his appreciation with that simple gesture. "I'm grateful for what you've done for us tonight, Luke, and I am sorry as hell that you were hurt."

But Janet's attention had shifted to Chinook. The stallion was terrified. The whites of his eyes flashed. His skin twitched. His entire body seemed to tremble. He bucked, kicked.

"Oh, you poor thing!" Without thinking, without asking anyone, Janet walked over to Chinook's stall, opened the sliding door, and stepped inside.

Jack helped Burt get Luke out of the barn, then turned toward Chinook—and his heart seemed to stop. "Janet!"

She'd gone into Chinook's stall, hooves slashing the air around her.

Jack ran toward her, then stopped, unable to believe what he was seeing.

Chinook quit rearing and bucking, his attention on Janet, who spoke to him in soothing tones, her arms at her sides.

"It's okay, boy. It's all right now."

Chuck glanced over at Jack, but didn't say a word, a look of shock on his face.

Jack walked slowly toward the stall, not wanting to startle the stallion with Janet so close to him. "Janet, honey, why don't you ease on out of there?"

She didn't answer, but continued to speak softly to the stallion. "I'm sorry. I know you're scared."

The horse whinnied, snorted, then walked over to Janet, still trembling.

"Good boy." She patted the animal's neck, took hold of his halter. "You're all sweaty. I don't want you to get chilled out here."

Jack stopped just outside the stall. "Chuck, go get Chinook's blanket and a curry comb and brush."

"Right, boss."

Janet crooned to the stallion, stroked him, and Jack could see Chinook calm under her touch, his trembling subsiding.

Then the stallion stretched his neck out toward her, lowering his muzzle almost to the straw in a gesture of affection and submission.

Well, I'll be damned.

"We ought to move him," Janet said. "The sheriff's department is going to need to come in here and take photos and comb the place for evidence. That won't be good for Chinook."

She was right.

Chuck returned, blanket over one arm, curry comb and brush in his hands. "Here you go, boss man."

Jack took the items from him. "Get the other stallion stall ready. We're going to have investigators tearing this place apart soon. We need to put Chinook somewhere he feels calm."

Chuck nodded. "I just can't believe Kip would do this. Yeah, he drank sometimes, but he was never the violent sort."

That thought had crossed Jack's mind, too. "Anger and pride can make a man do some pretty foolish things."

"That's true enough." Chuck hurried off.

Jack carefully and quietly entered Chinook's stall, draped the blanket through the feed opening, then handed Janet the curry comb. "You didn't tell me you were a horse whisperer."

"I'm not—at least I don't think I am."

"Well, you nearly gave me a heart attack. If you were one of my men, I'd fire you on the spot for being reckless."

"I'm not one of your men."

"Thank God for that." Still, he needed to make his point. "You could have been killed. I've seen stallions go crazy and injure experienced horsemen, men who raised them. You took a real chance stepping in here."

"I'm sorry I frightened you. I saw how afraid Chinook was, and I just had to do something."

He handed her the curry comb. "Most people who saw a stallion in that state would see only aggression and feel afraid. But you saw that the stallion was afraid, and so you had no fear. You amaze me."

She looked up at him and smiled. "That goes both ways."

He was glad to hear that. In the course of the evening, he'd come to realize that he loved her. For the second time in his life, he'd fallen head over heels in love with a woman.

CHAPTER EIGHT

J anet helped Jack rub down Chinook, then watched as he and Chuck
got the stallion settled in a stall on the other side of the building.

"I'll stay with him tonight, boss."

"Thanks, Chuck. Stay sharp. I'm walking Ms. Killeen back inside."

Janet wasn't used to feeling protected. She was used to being the one
doing the protecting. Having a man fuss over her like this felt strange, but
it also felt good. If given the chance, she might even be able to get used to
it.

Jack walked over to her, took her arm in his as they left the stables.
His voice was calm, but Janet could feel his rage. One of his men had been
shot, almost killed, and his prize stallion had again been threatened. He felt
responsible. "Burt and I are taking Luke to the hospital in Scarlet.
Detective Sergeant Taylor is meeting us there. As soon as I've paid the bill
and Luke has given a statement, I'll catch a ride back home with Taylor.
He wants to search the scene for evidence tonight. Burt and Luke will
come back in the truck when Luke is released. It's going to be a long night.
You should get some rest."

"It doesn't feel right to me to crawl into bed with all of this going
on."

They stopped in the mudroom, and he helped her out of her parka. "I'm sure it must be hard for you to sit things out, but you didn't get much sleep last night."

"I'm not sure I *can* sleep."

"Try." He hung her coat on a hook. "I'll be back as soon as I can."

Janet watched him leave, took off her boots, and walked into the kitchen, where she made a pot of coffee—not the wisest course of action if she wanted to sleep. But who was she fooling? She wasn't going to sleep with Jack gone and a shooter on the loose.

She carried her cup of coffee into the living room, stood there for a moment just looking around. It felt strange to be alone in the big house. She walked toward the fireplace, drawn by photographs on the mantel. One showed Jack standing with Nate and a woman who must have been Theresa. The three of them radiated happiness, their love for one another apparent.

Nate, who was in full dress uniform, had his father's jaw and blue eyes, but he'd gotten his cheekbones from his mother. Jack looked younger with less gray in his hair and fewer lines around the eyes. But it was Theresa who drew and held Janet's gaze.

Janet could see why Jack had been attracted to her. She'd been a beautiful woman, her delicate features ageless, her bearing sophisticated, her hazel eyes warm and full of life. This house had been *her* home. Jack had been *her* husband.

What am I doing here?

Janet had no business starting a relationship with anyone. She ought to be focused on getting her life back together, not allowing herself to be distracted by the first handsome man to show her kindness.

Then again, she'd come up here to relax and celebrate finishing rehab. Was it so wrong to enjoy Jack's hospitality and his company?

No, damn it. It wasn't.

Feeling on edge, she carried her coffee cup to the kitchen sink, went to her room, and filled the big bathtub with hot water, hoping to soak both the tension and her aches and pains away. She sank into the hot water with a sigh and let her mind wander, the heat immediately soothing to her sore muscles.

She found herself thinking over the case. It was just habit. Before the shooting, she'd often ended the day by relaxing in the tub and mulling over the details of whatever case she was handling. Except this wasn't a case— or it wasn't *her* case. Still, she couldn't get it out of her head, the details drifting through her thoughts.

Chinook screaming in his stall. Luke shaking, fighting tears, a deep graze in his shoulder. An angry ex-employee trying to settle the score with Jack.

Janet hoped they went after this Kip and brought him in for questioning. She wanted him behind bars, where he couldn't hurt Jack.

She let the tub drain, dried off with a fluffy towel, then slipped into her pajamas, crawled into bed, and was instantly fast asleep.

It was four in the morning when Jack walked into the house. He took off his gloves, parka, and boots, stopped for a drink of water in the dark kitchen, and headed for his bedroom, mind and body exhausted. Luke had identified Kip from his DMV photo in a photo lineup of six other random men. The kid had never met Kip. If that wasn't conclusive evidence, Jack didn't know what was. Luke had a deep flesh wound, but thankfully it wasn't serious. He'd be coming home in the morning.

Jack had ridden back with Det. Sgt. Taylor and had watched as Taylor and his team scoured the area around the stables and Chinook's stall for evidence. They'd found a .45 slug buried in the east wall behind Luke's cot. They'd found two shell casings—both 9mm from Luke's Glock 17—and a single .45 casing near the stable door, presumably from Kip's weapon.

Like Chuck, Jack was surprised that Kip could do anything as despicable as shoot man or horse. Then again, human beings were nature's least predictable animal.

As he passed Janet's room, he noticed light coming from beneath her door. He tapped lightly. "Janet, honey? Are you okay?"

The moment she opened the door, he could see she wasn't. There were tear stains on her cheeks, and her eyes were red. He was proud of himself for seeing both of these things before noticing how sweet and sexy she looked in her silk nightgown.

You are the soul of decency and decorum, West.

She kept her face averted, as if to hide her distress from him. "I'm fine. I'm just having a bit of a rough night."

"You're having nightmares again, aren't you?" He'd worried that tonight's shooting would trigger her again.

She nodded, her chin quivering. "Every time I close my eyes ... "

"It was selfish of me to ask you to stay here with all of this going on. I should have taken you back to Denver today when the highway reopened."

She pressed her fingertips to his lips to silence him. "Please don't say that. I've had a great time."

"Give me a few minutes to get washed up, and I'll make you my special remedy for sleepless nights."

"I don't want you to go to any trouble."

He reached out, ran his knuckles over her cheek. "Just say, 'Thank you.'"

"Thank you." She smiled.

He hit the shower, brushed his teeth, then dressed in a T-shirt and pair of sweatpants and walked to the kitchen, where he found Janet reading yesterday's paper, a silk robe covering her nightgown, her feet bare.

She looked up. "How did it go tonight?"

While he heated milk in a saucepan on the stove, he brought her up to date. "Luke identified Kip from a photo lineup. Taylor says they're going to bring Kip in tomorrow morning. As soon as they get a warrant, they'll search his place for firearms. I wouldn't have thought him capable of this, but I guess you never know."

"Why did you fire him?"

"He had a drinking problem. He never got violent, but he did have a hard time presenting himself for work in the morning. We gave him a few warnings. I even gave him time off to go to alcohol treatment. But a few weeks ago, he missed his shift again. I had to draw the line somewhere."

"Was he resentful about being fired?"

"Not that I could tell. But enough already. I don't want you worrying about any of this." Jack took the mug from the microwave, sprinkled a bit of nutmeg into the milk. "Now we're ready for the secret ingredient."

"Is that secret ingredient some form of booze?" Her lips curved into a smile.

"Damn it, how did you know? It must be your special agent training."

She laughed. "Bourbon was the secret ingredient in your chili. Hard cider was the secret ingredient in your stew. Let's just say I made an educated guess."

"I feel transparent, exposed." He got down a bottle of Aberfeldy, poured out a shot, and stirred it into the warm milk. "It's bedtime. Let's get back to your room."

She pointed to the mug, confusion on her pretty face. "Shouldn't I drink that concoction first?"

He shook his head. "You're going to be asleep thirty seconds after you drink this, so unless you want to sleep on the floor ... "

She gave him a look that said she didn't believe him but grabbed her cane, got to her feet, and started down the hallway.

When they reached her room, she slipped off her bathrobe and sat on the edge of the bed, staring skeptically at the mug in his hand.

He handed her the mug. "Drink it as fast as you can."

She took a sip, made a face, shuddered. "Oh, God! That's *awful!*"

"I didn't say it would taste good. Drink."

She took a breath, clearly gathering her resolve, then swallowed the drink in several deep gulps and shuddered. "Oooh, God!"

He couldn't help but laugh. "I'm right down the hall if you need me. You know which room is mine, right?"

"Yes." She looked up at him, her gaze slowly losing focus, then lay back on her pillows. "But Jack..."

"Yeah?" He drew the blankets and quilt up over her.

She caught one of his hands with her much smaller one, her eyes drifting shut. "Can't you stay? Not for sex, though I like the thought of having sex with you. It's just that I don't think I'll ... have bad dreams ... if you're ... with ... me."

He didn't think she'd dream regardless, but he didn't say that. He reached up, brushed a dark strand of hair from her cheek. "Sure. I'll be right here."

When he was certain she was asleep, he went to grab a throw blanket off the sofa in his bedroom, then stretched out on the chaise longue beside her bed. It was a chaise not-nearly-long-enough, if you asked him.

He glanced over at Janet, thought about what she'd revealed.

So, she liked the idea of having sex with him, huh? Well, he couldn't fathom how that could be true, given how much older he was, but as they said, *"In vino veritas."* It was a fortunate coincidence, because he liked the idea of having sex with her, too.

On that thought, he closed his eyes.

Janet stretched and rolled over, feeling wonderfully rested, her mind blank. She opened her eyes, looked around the comfortable little room that had become her home away from home, then glanced at the clock on her nightstand. She sat bolt upright.

How could it possibly be 11:45 already?

She got up, brushed her teeth and her hair, washed her face, then put on her makeup and got dressed, her gaze falling on the chaise longue. It sat up against the bed, a blanket she hadn't seen before draped across it.

Can't you stay?

She remembered herself saying those words.

Jack must have slept there.

That couldn't have been comfortable. He was a tall man, well over six feet. Still, he'd been too much of a gentleman to sleep in her bed when she was drugged on his hideous concoction, so he'd slept in the chair.

The thought warmed her. What a caring, unselfish man he was.

Not that she would object to sharing a bed with him, but she'd prefer to be awake if and when it actually happened.

I like the thought of having sex with you.

Oh, God! Had she really said that?

Fantastic.

Even as she wrestled with her own embarrassment, she knew Jack wouldn't throw her words in her face or use them to pressure her. He wasn't that kind of man.

She checked her appearance and saw a light in her eyes that hadn't been there in a long time. She was *happy*. She was actually happy again. And it wasn't a mystery why.

She left her room and walked to the kitchen, where she found a pot of coffee waiting for her along with a handwritten note.

I'm out with the horses. Breakfast is waiting for you in the buffet server. Help yourself. I hope you slept well.

Yours,

Jack

She lifted the lids on the little electric buffet server and found scrambled eggs, bacon, sausage links, and cinnamon French toast. Her mouth watered at the mingled scents. French toast had been a favorite of hers since she'd been a little girl.

She piled her plate embarrassingly high, then went to the table, where she found butter and—*yes!*—real maple syrup. How anyone ate the other kind, she couldn't say.

She'd savored the food, allowed herself to eat an extra piece of sausage, and then another, then put her dishes in the dishwasher and started the machine. She'd just poured herself another cup of coffee, when Jack walked in.

He smiled when he saw her, and her heart did a little flip. "Good morning, beautiful. How did you sleep?"

She felt heat in her cheeks. "I slept well, thank you. Thanks for staying with me. Did you get any sleep in that chair?"

"Oh, yeah." He reached for a coffee cup. "I can sleep pretty much anywhere—a benefit of having served with the Rangers. If I get five hours a night, I'm good."

She poured the coffee for him. "Is there any news?"

"As a matter of fact, I just heard from Taylor." He sat at the table. "Police picked up Kip first thing this morning."

"Thank goodness." A warm sense of relief rushed through her.

The man was in custody and no longer a threat.

Jack went on. "He denies shooting Chinook or Luke, claims he was home drunk both nights."

She poured milk into her coffee and stirred. "Can anyone corroborate that?"

Jack shook his head. "They searched his place and found three forty-fives, including a Kimber 1911. I don't know if it's the same one that was reported stolen. They've sent off all of the weapons for ballistics testing."

"Was he up there with you the day you confronted the hunters? I thought that happened a few days before the blizzard. You said you fired Kip a few weeks ago."

"You're right. He was fired last month, but that doesn't mean he wasn't there. He knows the property like the back of his hand. He could have followed us, hung back in the trees, and taken the weapon while we were all distracted."

She supposed that was as good an explanation as any. "I guess we just have to wait for the ballistics tests."

Jack frowned, got to his feet. "I don't want you thinking about all of this. When you finish your coffee, we're heading out to those stables. Today, you're riding Buckwheat on your own."

"You'll help me mount and dismount, right?"

"You bet—if you want me to."

Thirty minutes later, she found herself walking up the stairs of the mounting block without her cane, Jack holding her right hand. Buckwheat watched her progress through a gentle, dark eye, his stillness a contrast to her nervousness.

Jack handed her the reins. "You can do this."

She took the reins and the saddle horn in her left hand, her pulse quickening. She looked down, lifted her left leg high, tried to get the tip of her unresponsive left foot into the stirrup once, twice, three times.

Buckwheat craned his neck to watch, but didn't move.

Janet tried again, resolved to ask Jack for help if she couldn't do it this time. She bent her knee again, lifted her leg higher, and her left foot slid into the stirrup. When she was certain her foot was where it should be, she straightened her leg and shifted her weight onto it, then lifted her right leg over the saddle.

She let out a relieved breath and found Jack smiling up at her. She couldn't help but smile back. "Okay, Buckwheat, let's go for a walk."

Jack never got tired of it. He never got tired of watching someone who'd been hurt in some way rediscover a sense of joy riding on the back of a horse. Buckwheat had helped his daughter-in-law recover from a hellish life, and now the gelding was giving Janet back a piece of herself that she'd thought she'd lost.

She walked Buckwheat around the riding barn, then brought him easily to a lope, her face alive with happiness. She rode with the skill of someone who'd been born to it, and although she'd been raised riding in the English fashion, she'd obviously become accustomed to riding Western style somewhere along the way. Buckwheat responded to her lightest touch, horse and rider seeming to move as one.

God, she was a sight. Just watching her made his heart beat faster. Did she have any idea how beautiful she was, or had a life of working in pantsuits and facing down society's violent assholes left her unaware of her own feminine appeal?

Can't you stay? Not for sex, though I like the thought of having sex with you.

He'd heard what she'd said last night, but he wasn't sure that was the direction she wanted to take things. She had yet to kiss him. He'd promised not to cross that line again until she did, and if she wasn't going to do it...

Hell.

Well, at least he knew she'd thought about it, and it was the thought that counted.

Keep telling yourself that.

She loped the horse again, then brought him to a gallop, giving him his head. Her laughter rang through the confined space, the sound of her joy bringing a smile to his face. She let the gelding run off his restlessness before reining him in and letting him walk it out. She smiled at him as she passed, patting Buckwheat on his neck. "What a sweet big boy you are."

She circled once more, then reined Buckwheat to a halt beside the mounting block. She reached out, handed Jack the reins. "Last time, I almost fell dismounting."

He was pretty sure she could do this without his help, but he wasn't about to deny her. "Just take your time."

She grasped the saddle horn, looked down at her left foot as if to see whether it was still where she'd put it. Then she lifted her right leg over the saddle, dismounting smoothly. Her gaze met his, surprise in her eyes as if she couldn't believe she'd done it on her own.

He started to say something encouraging, but then she was in his arms, her mouth on his, her arms locked behind his neck.

He dropped Buckwheat's reins, wrapped his arms around her, crushed her against him, the need he felt for her, need he'd suppressed, rising fast and wild in his blood. He let her take the lead, answering the flick of her tongue with his, tasting her lips when she tasted his, breathing in when she exhaled. God, she tasted sweet, her body soft and precious in his arms.

Somewhere very nearby, a horse snorted, and he felt something nibbling at his coat. Reluctantly, he ended the kiss and found Buckwheat nipping his pocket to check for carrots. "Hey, knock that off."

Janet laughed, patted the horse's neck. "I suppose he wants attention, too."

"Yeah, well, I'm sure as hell not kissing him."

She laughed again, her gaze meeting his. "Thank you, Jack."

"You do realize you kissed me, right? You know what that means."

She smiled, the seductive glint in her eyes making his heart skip a beat. "I guess you have no choice now but to kiss me back."

He had no choice. No choice at all.

CHAPTER NINE

Jack wasn't on vacation like Janet was. With Luke recovering and Nate still in Denver, he had a full afternoon of work cut out for him in the stables. Janet stayed with him as he went from stall to stall, checking on the health of the mares and yearling foals, turning them over to Chuck to exercise in the riding barn, then shoveling manure and dirty straw into a large wheelbarrow while the stalls were empty.

She had a feeling he could have asked one of his men to do this but chose to do it himself. It was part of the way he held their respect. There was probably no job on the ranch he hadn't done, no job he felt was beneath him. How could any of his men shirk their duties when he worked so hard?

"I don't know why a woman with as much sense as you wants to stand out here in the cold watching me shovel straw and horseshit," he said.

But Janet knew that he *did* understand.

She wanted to be near the horses, near the way of life she'd known as a child, but she also wanted to be near *him*. It didn't matter what he was doing. She just wanted to be close to him. In truth, she couldn't get enough of him, couldn't get enough of his voice, his wit, couldn't get enough of watching him, of watching the way his body moved.

Of course, what she *really* wanted was to kiss him again. She was pretty sure he knew that, too. But now wasn't the best time, and the stables certainly weren't the place.

She helped as much as she could, distributing clean straw and fresh hay, holding a skittish yearling colt by its halter while Jack dealt with a problem with the stall door latch. They talked about horses, about his service in Vietnam, about her new position.

"It sounds like a promotion."

"Technically, it is."

"Are you excited to get started?"

"No. I'm dreading it. I never wanted to work a desk job. I like being outside. I know being on the city streets probably doesn't sound to you like being out of doors, but it's a lot better than sitting on your butt in a big glass and concrete box, breathing canned air and staring at a computer all day."

"I'd have to agree with you there." He pushed the very full wheelbarrow to the next empty stall. "Have you thought about retiring early?"

"I've thought about it. I would lose a fair amount of my pension if I did. Besides, what would I do with myself?"

"You could work for me."

"Work ... as a ranch hand?" She laughed, genuinely amused by the image of herself in a cowboy hat cutting cattle that popped into her head. "I can't even walk in the snow without help."

He glared at her. "You're a fantastic rider."

She narrowed her eyes at him. "Are you truly offering me a job?"

He stopped shoveling, rested on the hay fork, gave her a lopsided grin. "I would if it would keep you around."

Something about that felt more romantic to her than a dozen red roses.

"Jack West, you are a charming man."

"Me?" He shook his head, got back to shoveling. "I think you need to look that word up in the dictionary, angel."

He stopped once to chat with one of his men, who was driving up to Scarlet Springs to pick up a few things. He handed the man a slip of paper. "Here's my list and explicit instructions. Get my credit card from Chuck."

"Yes, sir."

He pushed the wheelbarrow outside, dumped it onto a concrete pad the size of the average living room. "We compost this and sell it to nearby organic farms. Between the cattle and the horses, we have no shortage of shit."

Janet laughed. "I suppose not."

She walked with him to the barn that held Chinook's stalls and watched while Jack checked the stallion's wound and then tacked him up.

"Nate and I are the only two who ride or exercise Chinook." He led the stallion toward the riding barn, Janet walking beside them.

"Has no one else ever ridden—" Janet's cane slipped on the ice, and she pitched forward with a cry.

But instead of hitting the ground, she found herself draped across Chinook's thick neck, his coarse mane tickling her chin. The stallion whickered softly, slowly raising his head and helping Janet back to her feet.

Stunned, she looked over at Jack. "Did he just do that on purpose?"

Jack looked from her to Chinook, clearly surprised, then patted the stallion's shoulder. "Like I always say—women and horses."

When they reached the riding barn, Janet realized she was in for a treat. She'd never seen anyone ride a stallion before.

"Are you ready to show off for Ms. Killeen, old boy?"

The stallion whinnied, tossed his head.

She stood back against the wall near the door where she wouldn't startle or distract the horse and watched as Jack climbed into the saddle. Having just spent the day around the other horses, she could now see how much more muscular Chinook was than the mares or even Buckwheat. The animal's body rippled with tension, his chest broader and his neck thicker than those of the other horses. She knew Chinook was capable of hurting or even killing a person, but as Jack urged the stallion to a walk and then a lope, there was no doubt which one of the two was in control.

She could have watched for hours, the grace of rider and horse truly something to behold, a lifetime of love and skill evident in Jack's absolute mastery of the animal, in his smooth motions, his flawless riding.

God, it turned her on.

What would he be like in bed? She couldn't help but remember what his thighs had felt like pressed against hers when they'd ridden together on Buckwheat. It took real strength and concentration to manage an animal of this size and vigor. Would he have that same control during sex?

Okay, now she was being ridiculous.

Then he rode by at a gallop and smiled to her, and she felt her ovaries explode.

But it didn't matter what her ovaries had to say. The situation was complicated. If she wanted to be intimate with Jack, she would have to tell him.

Somehow, she would have to tell him everything.

J ack stood in front of his mirror, adjusted his tie, studied his
reflection. He'd showered, shaved, even changed his sheets. He
supposed he looked decent enough for a man his age. His tails still
fit, which was something.

What in the hell have you gotten yourself into, amigo?

Hell, he didn't know, but he wasn't going to retreat. He had feelings
for Janet, and she had feelings for him. She was attracted to him. The kiss
in the riding barn had made that clear. And God knew he was attracted to
her.

There was a lot more gray in his hair than there had been the last time
he'd set out to seduce a woman—and more lines on his face. He'd been
eighteen then and as full of himself as any young man could be. He'd been
the star quarterback, the sole heir of the Cimarron, and popular enough that
he'd never lacked for male friends or female attention. He'd set his sights
on Theresa, and for some reason, she'd wanted him, too.

He knew their first time hadn't been good for her. He hadn't known
what the hell he was doing, and she'd been a virgin. It had taken Vietnam
to pull his head out of his ass and teach him humility. Even so, it hadn't
been until after Nate was born that he'd learned how to love Theresa the
way she deserved to be loved—and how to satisfy her fully in bed. Women
were so very different from men.

Not that he and Janet were going to have sex tonight. He didn't want
to rush her, didn't want to ruin their relationship by becoming too intimate
too soon. Still, if things went in that direction, he wouldn't mind at all.

He'd come up with this plan this morning while watching her sleep. A
romantic dinner. Maybe some dancing.

"Go explore the library and then pamper yourself for a while," he'd told her after they'd finished rubbing down Chinook. "And dress for dinner tonight."

"Dress for dinner? You mean like on *Downton Abbey*?"

"Downtown what?" he'd joked. "Yeah, like that."

Megan was obsessed with the show, so of course he'd heard of it.

"I didn't pack anything formal."

"I've taken care of that." He'd stolen a few moments when she'd been asleep to order a gown and flowers and have them delivered, along with groceries and even condoms. "There's a surprise waiting for you in your room."

The delight on her face had made him smile.

Now, dinner was done. A maple cream pie was chilling in the fridge along with the wine. It was time.

He ran his hands down the panels of his dress coat, making sure every detail was correct. He wasn't uncomfortable in suits the way some men were. He'd worn a military uniform for six years, and that's what a suit was—a kind of uniform.

He drew a breath, tried to settle his nerves, then walked down the hallway past her closed bedroom door and got busy laying out the table. He'd almost finished setting the places, when he remembered that this was Theresa's favorite set of china. He'd bought it for her one Christmas. They'd saved it for special occasions.

He stopped, closed his eyes.

I love you, Theresa, and I'll never forget you. But I love her, too.

It's okay, Jack. She's a beautiful woman. I like her, and I want you to be happy.

He heard Theresa's voice as if she were standing right there beside him. His throat went tight.

Ah, hell.

He hadn't heard her voice for seven long years and had surely imagined it now. It was probably just his mind playing tricks on him. Still, any doubts he might have had about the rightness of what he was doing faded. Theresa *would* want him to be happy. She'd loved him that much, not a selfish bone in her body.

He got out the good silver, took down the crystal—white wine glasses, water glasses, port glasses. Then he set the bouquet of flowers in place, started the music—Bach's cello suites—and lit the candles. He'd just carried the serving trays to the table when she appeared.

The breath left his lungs in a rush. "You look ... *beautiful.*"

The gown fit her perfectly, its V-neck revealing a hint of cleavage, its bodice covered with beads and glittery stuff, the pale rose-colored silk suiting her dark hair and green eyes. She'd put her hair up into some kind of elegant twist and wore simple pearls on her earlobes. But it was her face Jack noticed most. She looked radiantly happy.

"The gown is so lovely. I've never worn anything like it. I feel like a fairytale princess." Smiling, she slowly turned so that he could see. "How did you know my size?"

He'd done a bit of research in her closet early this morning, but he wasn't going to tell her that. "Just a lucky guess."

"You did all of this? This is beautiful china." She touched a finger to the platinum trim on one of the plates, then bent down to sniff a rose. "Mmm. Heavenly."

"I'm glad you like it." He drew out her chair. "Dinner is ready."

"That smells incredible."

"Chicken Saltimbocca. It's a favorite of mine." He served the meal, poured the wine, then sat across from her. "I'm a simple man, Janet. I say what I mean and have no talent for games. I want to show you how I feel about you so there's no chance for misunderstanding. If you think I'm trying to romance you, you're right. I am."

"Oh, Jack." She smiled, raised her glass. "It's working. Cheers."

J anet rested her head on Jack's chest, her blood warmed by good food, wine and conversation, her body moving with his as they slow-danced in the broad entryway to the living room. Her cane rested against the wall, forgotten, his arms holding her steady as they swayed in time to the music. Percy Sledge had just finished "When a Man Loves a Woman," and the Righteous Brothers were now singing "Unchained Melody."

She barely heard the lyrics, aware only of Jack. The thrum of his heartbeat beneath her cheek. The hardness of his chest. The subtlest motions of his body. The scents that surrounded him—the spice of his skin, the starch of his shirt, the dark amber tone of his cologne.

She tilted her head, looked up at him. "When are you going to kiss me?"

"Right about now." He brushed his lips lightly over hers again and again until her own lips burned and she thought she might go crazy. Then at last he claimed her mouth with a slow, deep kiss that brought their dance to a standstill, one big hand sliding slowly up her spine, the other holding her close.

Janet's body seemed to come alive under the magic of that kiss, her pulse racing, need for him flaring inside her. She locked her arms behind his neck and kissed him back.

He moaned and slid a hand into her hair, scattering her hairpins and destroying her chignon as he tilted her head back to expose her throat, his lips pressing kisses against the sensitive skin beneath her ear. She yielded to the thrill of his touch as he licked and nipped a path over her skin, leaving goose bumps in his wake, making her shiver.

He drew back, looked down at her. "Tell me if I'm going too fast."

"What if you're not going fast enough?"

His blue eyes went dark, and his mouth claimed hers again, this kiss fierce and unrestrained, his mouth consuming her, one hand sliding up to cup her breast through the beaded silk of her bodice.

Janet's knees went weak, wetness gathering between her thighs.

In one motion, he scooped her into his arms and carried her toward his bedroom. She was so swept up in her emotions, so swept up in him, that it took a moment for her to realize what she'd said and how he'd taken it.

She would have to tell him everything—now.

He set her on her feet next to his king-sized bed, letting her body slide down the length of his, the feel of his erection sending sparks through her belly.

"Jack, I'm sorry. But I ... " This wasn't going to be easy. "There's something I need to tell you."

"Now?"

"Yes."

He slid his fingers through hers, led her over to the sofa that sat in front of the fireplace, and drew her down beside him. "I'm listening."

She took a moment to prepare herself. She didn't need to be emotional about this. She could talk about it like she did any other case, any other crime. It didn't have to be her life she was talking about. Except that it was.

"You know I was shot, right?"

"Yes." His thumb smoothed circles over the back of her hand.

"The bullet that hit me was a 7.62 NATO armor piercing round."

He squeezed his eyes shut for a moment. "I didn't know that."

"The round entered through the back of my left hip, missing my femoral artery, but shattering my hip, severing my sciatic nerve and fracturing my pelvis before exiting in front." She fisted her free hand in her lap, her body beginning to tremble. "That's why I can't control my left foot."

"Hey, come here. You're shaking like a leaf." He wrapped his arm around her shoulder, drew her into the shelter of his embrace. "Just breathe."

She drew a few slow, deep breaths.

"That's better. Just take your time."

No emotion. Just the facts.

"The shock wave of the round tore my vaginal muscles, too."

"*God.*" The word was a whisper.

She wasn't even sure he'd meant to say it aloud or meant her to hear it.

"Surgeons replaced my entire hip joint, used plates and screws to put my pelvis back together, and reconnected my sciatic nerve. They were able to stitch everything else together, too, but... " She'd come to the really hard part now, and the words spilled out of her in a rush. "I don't know if it all works. I don't know how much function I have. I don't know if I can enjoy sex. I don't know if it will hurt. I ... I just don't know."

Jack traced lazy lines over her shoulder with his fingertips. "Did the doctors have any advice for you?"

"They told me I'd lost muscle and would be very tight. They said that sex might be painful and that I should expect some level of dysfunction, but they weren't specific."

"You haven't experimented, tried to answer those questions yourself?"

Heat rushed into her cheeks. "I ... um, no. I just never... That is to say, I don't..."

Jack shifted so that he faced her, cupped her cheek in a callused palm. "I'm so sorry for what you've been through. But I'm not Byron. I'm not going to turn away from you or pressure you into doing anything you're not ready to do. This is about what *you* need. If you want my help figuring things out, seeing what works and what doesn't, I'm ready and willing. I want you, Janet. I won't lie about that. But I sure as hell don't want to do anything that causes you pain or makes you unhappy."

"Oh, Jack." Relief flooded through her, along with a rush of tenderness for him. She knew he meant every word he'd said. "I *do* want you. I want you so badly."

"That's all I needed to hear. We'll figure the rest of it out along the way." Then he leaned in and kissed her.

CHAPTER TEN

J ack broke the kiss, looked down at Janet. "I think we'd both be more comfortable if we moved this to the bed."

She smiled, her lips wet from kissing him. "I like the way you think."

He drew her to her feet, helped her walk the short distance, willing himself to ignore his own anger and to focus only on the sweet woman who was trusting him with her body and soul tonight. He wouldn't be any good to her if he wasted his energy hating the man who'd shot her. The bastard was dead.

He drew her onto the bed beside him, ran his knuckles over the smooth curve of her cheek, her skin so soft. "We're going to take this nice and easy. Tell me when I'm getting it right, okay?"

She slid a hand into his hair and drew his lips toward hers. "So far, so very good."

That was reassuring to hear. It had been seven long, lonely years since he'd held a woman, seven years since he'd kissed a woman, and he worried that being out of practice might make him clumsy. But she wasn't complaining. Far from it.

Her fingers curled in the hair at his nape, her body arching against his as they kissed. He let himself go, tasting his way over her cheek and down the column of her throat. He felt the ragged beating of her pulse beneath his lips, watched her skin tighten into goose bumps, her responsiveness gratifying.

He slid a hand inside her gown, cupped her breast, its softness precious against his palm. He nibbled his way across her collarbone and kissed the divot at the base of her throat, his fingers plucking and teasing the petal softness of her nipple to a tight point. She gave a quick little gasp, arching into his hand.

Blood surged to his groin.

"Let's get this out of the way." He wanted to see, taste and touch every inch of her skin, her body so different from his.

Her eyes fluttered open, and she sat up, her dark hair spilling around her shoulders. "My zipper."

"I've got it." He reached behind her, found her zipper tab, worked it down, then tugged the gown down to her waist and unfastened her black lace bra.

A jolt of pure lust shot through him, two beautiful, natural breasts spilling into his hands, dusky pink nipples puckered into tight buds.

He rubbed his thumbs over their tips. "You are beautiful."

She reached over, fumbled with his tie. "I want to touch you, too."

"That seems fair." He took over for her, making short work of the tie, tossing the dress coat over a nearby chair, then removing his waistcoat and shirt with all of its damnable buttons and cuff links.

He watched as her gaze traveled over him, gave her time to explore. She pressed her palms against his chest, caressed his pecs and abs, her dilated pupils and her rapid breathing telling him that she liked what she saw. He pressed one of her hands against the place where his heart was pounding so hard and bore her back onto the bed. Then he let himself feast, suckling first one nipple and then the other, flicking their tips with his tongue, grazing her puckered areolas with his teeth, tugging on them with his lips.

She gasped, moaned, arched upward, her nails digging into his bicep.

He kept it up until she was panting, her eyes squeezed shut, her hips shifting on the bed. "Oh, you are sensitive, aren't you?"

Her eyes fluttered open again, and she looked at him, confused. "Hmm?"

She was just *that* far gone.

Good.

He chuckled, lowering his mouth to kiss and lick the skin beneath one breast, teasing the other with his palm. While his mouth stayed busy, he let his hand wander, let it skim over her ribcage and belly, savoring the satin feel of her skin and the way her muscles tensed at his touch.

He had to get her the rest of the way out of this damned gown, but that meant venturing into sensitive territory. "I want you naked. Are you okay with that?"

"Mmm, yes! But…"

He waited for her to finish.

"I don't wax or shave like a lot of women do these days."

He laughed. "Good. I don't want to feel like I'm having sex with a 10-year-old. I came of age in the seventies, when natural was sexy. I like bush."

She laughed, watching him as he finished undressing her, tossed her gown across the chair on top of his dress coat, and tugged off her black lace panties.

And he saw. "Oh, angel."

There was an angry red scar that ran the width of her lower belly, another that curved from her left buttock halfway down the outside of her thigh. There was a quarter-sized scar where the bullet had entered her body and a fist-sized scar in the crease of her hip in front where it had exited, taking flesh with it.

The rage he'd fought to subdue flared to life again. He reacted on instinct, sliding down to stroke and kiss his way over her scars, wanting so very much to take away the months of pain and suffering this single act of violence had brought her. He could change nothing, of course, but he *could* reassure her that none of this bothered him. She was nothing less than a hero in his eyes.

She sat up, a smile on her lips, a sheen of tears in her eyes. "You are so sweet."

Then her eyes narrowed. "Hey, why are you still wearing pants?"

"A foolish oversight, I assure you." He wrestled with his emotions, fighting back his rage once more, trying to be the man she needed tonight.

He wasn't ashamed of his body. He undressed slowly, letting her look her fill as he took off his shoes, pulled off his socks, then unzipped his trousers and removed them together with his boxer briefs. Her gaze was fixed on his cock, which grew harder under the heat of her perusal.

"Is that better?"

"Oh, that's *so* much better."

Janet stared at Jack's body, felt a flutter deep in her belly, desire for him turning to liquid between her thighs. The man might be sixty-three, but he was ripped. His broad chest was sprinkled with salt-

and-pepper curls, his shoulders, arms, chest, abdomen, and thighs all lean muscle, his cock jutting upward, thick and hard.

Oh, she wanted him.

A year ago, it would have been so simple. But now...

She reached for him, and he came to her, stretching out beside her, his gaze sliding over her, his hand caressing her from her breasts to her belly, his touch so very arousing. "Tell me if anything I do hurts."

"Just don't stop unless I say stop."

"Deal." He moved his body closer and parted her thighs, lifting her right leg so that it draped over his hip, opening her to his touch. "I need a little room here so I can get to know you."

His words sent anticipation shivering through her, his erection pressing hot and insistent against her right hip, his fingers tracing circles over the sensitive skin of her inner thighs. Then he lowered his mouth to her breasts and began to suckle her again.

It was such sweet torture, every tug of his lips, every flick of his tongue, every nip of his teeth sending sparks into her belly until she wanted to scream.

"Jack, you're *killing* me."

"Am I?" He sounded amused, his voice deep.

Then the hand that had been tickling her inner thighs moved to cup her. The pressure felt so good, his fingers parting her labia to explore her, teasing her and playing with her before finally settling on her clitoris, flicking, stroking, and ... *Oh*!

"Just ... like ... *that*."

The man knew what he was doing. She'd give him that. The combined sensations of his mouth and busy fingers were almost more than she could take, her body aching to be filled, the fire he'd built inside her begging to be quenched.

Somehow she managed to speak. "I want you … *inside*."

"Yeah?" He shifted his hand, one of his fingers making slick circles around the entrance to her vagina. "You are so wet. I can't wait to taste you here."

His words made her pulse skip.

Then, slowly, so slowly, he slid a finger, then two, inside her. There was no pain, only pleasure as he answered her yearning with slow, slick strokes. The fears Janet had carried for so long began to unravel as her body took over, Jack's skilled touch driving her toward the edge.

He shifted from one nipple to the other, whispering against her burning skin on the way, the vibrations of his voice seeming to pass through her. "I want to feel you come. Come around my fingers."

His words were like an aphrodisiac. Not that she needed one. She was already drunk on sex, her body hovering on the shimmering brink of an orgasm. It seemed like an eternity since she'd felt like this, so strung out… wanting him… wanting…

She came with a cry, climax surging through her in a rush of bliss, his fingers drawing out her pleasure until she lay weak and panting. She opened her eyes, found him watching her, a smile on his handsome face.

"Welcome back, angel."

"Jack." She reached up, caressed his cheek. "You're incredible."

He nuzzled her ear, a tender gesture that made her belly flutter. "The pleasure was mine, believe me."

Then he lowered his mouth to hers and kissed her, a slow, sweet kiss. And the fire he'd just extinguished flared to life again.

She reached down, took his cock in her hand, stroked the hard length of him, felt the muscles of his belly contract. "I want you inside me."

He twisted and reached for something—a box of condoms.

"You don't have to do that. Menopause hits the women in my family early. I haven't had a period in ten months. I mean… at my age? It's not going to happen."

"If you're sure."

She smiled, gave his cock a gentle tug, spread her legs. "Come here."

"Yes, ma'am." He settled himself between her thighs, lifting her left leg carefully, opening her legs wider. "How does that feel?"

A tinge of pain shot through her thigh, making her wince.

"Maybe put this beneath it." She reached for a pillow.

He did as she'd suggested, tucking the pillow beneath the bend of her knee. "How's that?"

"Good." She stroked him, savored the feel of his erection in her hand.

He let her play, his muscles tense as he held himself still above her, his blue eyes dark, the intensity in his gaze making her breath catch.

She guided him to her vagina, let him take it from there.

"Tell me if it hurts." He nudged himself inch by inch into her. "When they said you'd be tight … they meant it. *Jesus.*"

It felt wonderful—until…

A muscle spasm made her gasp, the pain sharp like a charley horse deep inside her. "Stop!"

Jack withdrew.

She closed her eyes, her heart sinking as the pain ebbed.

He kissed her cheek. "We don't have to do this. There are a lot of ways we can enjoy each other that don't involve my being inside you."

But she didn't want to surrender this part of her sexuality to a bullet. "Please. I don't want to give this up. Can we try again?"

"I don't want to cause you pain. It hurts me to see you hurt."

"Maybe if you don't go deep… "

"Relax, honey." He slid a finger inside her, caressed her.

She closed her eyes, willed her pelvic floor muscles to relax.

"That's better."

She grew aroused again, his persistent motions like an internal massage—a very erotic and stimulating massage.

He withdrew his finger, caught her right leg behind her knee, brought it up toward her shoulder, opening her more fully. "Just relax."

He nudged the head of his cock inside her, then withdrew. Again and again he entered her, going a little deeper each time before withdrawing. Where there had been pain, there was now only pleasure.

"Oh, Jack, *don't… stop.*"

J ack kept the rhythm slow and easy, sliding in and out of her heat. He couldn't stop himself from kissing her, his lips hungry for her mouth, her cheeks, her throat, her breasts. He was lost in her—the hot, tight feel of her, the musky scent of her arousal, the taste of her skin.

He wanted to last, wanted to make her come again, but it had been so long, so damned long. She felt like heaven, so perfect. He willed himself to slow down, to focus on her and not the sensation of being inside her, shifting to ride her higher, the base of his cock rubbing against her swollen little clit with each thrust.

She gave a little gasp, her nails digging into his back, her inner muscles drawing tighter. "Oh, that feels … *so* … good."

It sure as hell did.

God, he'd missed sex. He'd missed intimacy. He'd missed touching and holding a woman. He'd missed all the sweet, feminine things a woman brought to a man's life. He'd missed having someone special who was only his to care about.

And he *did* care about her. God help him, but in the span of just a few days, she'd come to mean the world to him.

Her eyes were closed now, her lips parted, her nails biting into his back, her breathing erratic, every exhalation a little moan.

He felt his balls draw tight, the first glimmer of orgasm uncoiling in his belly, the snug, slick friction driving him to the brink. He fought to relax, to hold on just a little longer, wanting to give her all the sexual pleasure he could. Then he felt the tension inside her peak and shatter.

Her breath broke, and she cried out his name, her back arching as she came, tears spilling down her cheeks. "Jack!"

He rode through it, kept his rhythm steady, her muscles clenching around him, drawing him over the edge. Orgasm rushed through him in a surge of blinding pleasure, searing him to his soul, his body shaking as he spilled himself inside her.

He gave himself a moment to catch his breath, kissing the tears from her cheeks, knowing without her needing to tell him why she was crying. She'd been afraid she'd lost this part of herself, but the two of them had proved that wrong.

Aware that he was still on top of her, he began to move.

She tightened her arms around him. "No. Not yet."

"I'm not too heavy?" He outweighed her by at least sixty pounds.

She smiled a sleepy smile, her eyes closed. "Not at all."

He rested his head against her breast, closed his eyes, listened to the soft thrum of her heartbeat, awash in soul-deep contentment. When he'd been a younger man, he'd thought the notion of a man and woman becoming one flesh was nothing more than words—fine, poetic words, to be true, but just words. It had taken him years to understand how his sexual bond with Theresa had changed him.

Now, lying in Janet's arms, he felt changed again—lighter, more alive, bound to her well-being and happiness as if it were his own.

His penis went soft and began to slide from her body.

She whimpered in protest. "No!"

Chuckling, he rolled onto his back and drew her into his arms, resting her head on his chest. "Don't worry, angel. There's more where that came from."

CHAPTER ELEVEN

Janet awoke to the delicious sensation of Jack's callused hand sliding over the bare skin of her ass.

"Good morning, angel." His voice was deep and sleepy. He nuzzled her ear, his hand squeezing her buttock then delving between her thighs from behind.

"Good morning." It felt wonderful—his fingers teasing her, sliding inside her, his erection pressing hard and hot against her.

He reached around to cup her breast, tugging her nipple to a tender point, the contact sending sparks of heat deep into her belly, making her inner muscles clench.

"Shouldn't you be up at the high pasture?" It was hard to think.

"I'm taking a day off."

"Good." She burned for him already. "Fuck me."

"Yes, ma'am." He nudged himself into her, thrusting slowly until he was deep inside her, his testicles brushing against her buttocks, the rhythmic penetration of his cock driving her straight toward orgasm.

"*Jack.*" She whispered his name, tried to reach for him, wanting to touch him. But in this position, with him behind her, almost on top of her, she could do nothing.

"Just lie there and enjoy."

If he'd been another man, his words might have been a meaningless boast. Oh, but he knew his way around a woman's body. He picked up the pace, forsaking her breast to reach beneath her and play with her clit. She fisted her hand in the sheet, the sensations he caused both unbearable and sweet.

Faster. Harder. He felt so good inside her, like steel in velvet, thick and hard.

Her hands bunched into fists, crumpled the sheet, beat against her pillow.

"God, woman, you feel so good."

She found herself arcing her lower back, trying to get more of him, her body teetering on the edge of bliss. And then it hit her, orgasm washing over her like a sunrise, scorching and bright. She bit her pillow, cried out, awash in pleasure as he maintained the rhythm, driving her climax home. Then he shuddered and moaned out her name, his breath hot against her nape as he came inside her.

For a moment, they lay there, both of them breathing hard.

"I wish I could wake up like this every day."

"You could." He ran his fingertips in lazy lines over the curve of her hip.

She smiled, remembering that he'd offered her a job. "Is that an employee benefit here at the ranch?"

He chuckled. "Not for most of the staff. Good God, now you've planted an image of Chuck in my head that I'm going to need a century to recover from."

She laughed, rolled over, wrapped her arms around his neck. "Your men will say I slept my way to the top."

"Jealous bitches." He kissed her nose. "Don't listen to them."

She laughed again, her heart feeling wide open, her soul alive, her blood like warm honey. "I adore you, Jack West."

"Well, that's a start." There was a teasing gleam in his blue eyes, but something in his voice told her there was more behind his words than he was letting show.

Was he in love with her?

The thought stunned her, sent her heart soaring.

Was she in love with him? How could she be? She'd only known him for a few short days—if you didn't count the past nine months she'd spent loathing him.

"I took the liberty of moving your things from the guest room to my bedroom while you were sleeping. I hope that's okay with you."

It was better than okay.

"Thank you. Now I don't have to figure out how to sneak my way in—you know, leaving my things in your bathroom bit by bit."

"You never have to sneak, Janet. Ask for what you want. Say what's on your mind. Be honest with me, and I'll always be honest with you."

What he was describing was the deepest form of intimacy.

She felt a hitch in her chest, touched by his openness. "You dear, sweet man."

"You take a shower, do whatever you do in the morning. I'll make us some breakfast."

"Won't you take a shower with me?"

He grinned. "I'd be happy to be your rubber duckie."

The master bathroom was a bigger, more beautiful version of the guest bathroom. It was easily the size of her living room, with an enormous sunken tub, a wide shower with multiple shower heads, his and her sinks, and radiant heat. An upholstered chaise sat at one end beside a corner table that held candles and magazines. Windows ran along the top of the wall, bringing daylight while allowing privacy.

"This is beautiful."

They stepped into the shower together. Jack massaged shampoo into her hair, rubbed soap over her breasts and between her thighs, then rinsed it all away, his touch and the hot water both soothing and erotic, her body still singing from their lovemaking. When she was squeaky clean, she returned the favor, even spreading shaving cream on his face so that he could shave.

Neither of them spoke. There seemed to be no need for words, a touch, a smile, a glance more than enough, their moans of pleasure and laughter mingling with the music of the water.

Jack made eggs Benedict and mimosas for breakfast with a little help from Janet. He showed her how to use the juicer to make orange juice, then made the Hollandaise himself. Fresh strawberries rounded out the meal, the two of them picking berries from the bowl and feeding each other by hand.

He felt like he was walking on air, almost unable to believe that this wonderful, beautiful woman was here with him, sharing this meal, his day, his bed.

You fell head first this time, amigo.

A voice inside him reminded him that they hadn't yet made each other a single promise and that there was every chance Janet would decide to walk out the door and never come back. She was eighteen years younger than he was, only nine years older than his son. What could she possibly see in him?

He told that voice to go to hell.

She cared for him, too. He knew it. She seemed to be as lost in the moment as he, smiling and laughing with an ease that hadn't been a part of her when she'd first arrived, exhausted and chilled to the bone. Her body responded to his touch as if she'd been made for him, which meant her heart and mind were in the game, too. Most of all, she'd trusted him with her worst fears. He'd lived long enough to know that a woman didn't do that with just any man.

They'd just cleared the dishes away when Sheriff Rove called.

"How are things, Mr. West?"

"All is well. Chinook is healing, and so is Luke."

Chuck said the kid was still bragging to anyone who would listen how he'd saved the stallion and frightened Kip away. It was starting to get on the men's nerves.

"I wanted to let you know Kip Henderson had his arraignment this morning. The district attorney threw the book at him—attempted first-degree murder, assault with intent to kill, assault with a deadly weapon, animal cruelty, destruction of property. There are a few more charges. I can't remember them all. If they convict him, he won't be seeing the outside of a prison cell anytime soon."

Jack had already heard this from the DA's office, but hearing it again, he found it sad to think that Kip had come to this end. "What a shame."

Rove went on. "You don't have to worry about him making bond. The judge set bail at five hundred grand."

Kip didn't have the collateral for that. He didn't even have a pot to piss in.

"Do you have the ballistics results back yet?"

"That could take months. Sometimes CBI takes a year to get results back to us."

"A year? That's ridiculous."

Janet shook her head, whispered, "Tell him to send them to the FBI. I'll file the paperwork and put in the request."

Jack nodded. "How about sending them to the FBI? Ms. Killeen is willing to do the paperwork and—"

"I don't see the point in troubling anyone or putting CBI's nose out of joint by turning to the feds. We have the guilty party in our jail. The man had motive, opportunity, and the ability to carry out the crime. We have an eyewitness. I'm not sure we even need the ballistics evidence to force a plea deal here."

Jack looked to Janet, shook his head. "Has Kip admitted to any of it?"

"No, he still says he didn't do it, but then if you ask around, you'll learn that no one in my jail is guilty."

Jack supposed that was true enough. "Has anyone notified his kin? Does he have any money in his commissary account?"

If he didn't, Jack would transfer some to him via his attorney. Now that the man was no longer a threat, Jack felt kind of sorry for him.

"I'm not sure." Sheriff Rove sounded surprised that Jack would care. "I could have the jail captain call you."

"I'd appreciate that."

"You're the county's biggest land owner, Mr. West. We want you to know we're on top of this case."

So this call had more to do with the sheriff's upcoming re-election campaign than it did Kip or Chinook or the law. God, Jack hated politics. "Keep me posted."

He turned to find Janet watching him.

"They won't turn to the Bureau for the ballistics testing?"

He shook his head. "Rove is afraid of ruffling feathers at CBI."

"That's absurd."

"That's politics."

"It's kind of you to want to help Kip, considering what he's done." She slid her arms around him, rested her head against his chest. "You really are a softie, aren't you?"

He held her fast, kissed her damp hair. "Don't tell anyone."

"Your secret is safe with me."

"It's beautiful." Janet could almost feel her soul sigh. Snug in her parka, a thick sheepskin on her lap, she looked around her. Tall aspens surrounded the sleigh, their leaves fluttering like so many gold coins in the breeze, their thick white trunks reaching skyward, making her feel as if she were sitting in a golden cathedral, its ceiling the endless blue dome of the sky.

"You said you wanted to see aspens." Jack's voice was soft, as if he, too, were moved by the beauty of this place. "You can see the house down there."

Janet shifted slightly in her seat, peered through the trees. "It looks so small. How high up are we?"

"We're at about ten thousand feet elevation or so." He started naming the mountains, pointing to each one, giving her the elevation of each summit. It was clear to Janet that this was a special place for him, someplace he'd been many times before. "I never get tired of this view."

"I don't think I would either."

"Good." He looked over at her, gave her a smile, his eyes hidden behind sunglasses, a black cowboy hat on his head.

They'd been gone for about an hour now, Jack holding the reins as Buckwheat pulled the sleigh along a gradual incline, the snow now compacted enough for the horse to manage. Janet had never ridden in a sleigh before but found she quite enjoyed it, the bells on Buckwheat's harness jingling merrily, the scenery rolling slowly by. Jack seemed to have a story for every bend in the road, every stand of trees, every frozen stream—where he'd had a tree fort, where he'd recently seen a mountain lion, where he'd shot his first buck, where his father had taken him to give him the "talk." And Janet had come to realize that Jack was as much a part of this land as any tree or lake.

The Cimarron was in his blood.

"It's so quiet."

Jack began to recite something. "The meadows and far-sheeted streams/Lie still without a sound/Like some soft minister of dreams/The snow-fall hoods me round/In wood and water, earth and air/A silence everywhere."

She stared at him, surprised. "Is that a poem?"

Jack nodded. "Archibald Lampman. I thought he really described what snow does to the landscape better than anyone. Then again, he was Canadian, so I bet he had lots of time to think about it."

She laughed. "I thought you needed whiskey for poetry."

He leaned over and kissed her. "Sometimes, I just get inspired."

He tied off the reins, reached down beneath the seat of the sleigh, and pulled out a thermos. "Hot chocolate?"

"You think of everything, don't you?" She'd known it was there—along with a loaded AR-15.

"I try." He opened the thermos, poured steaming chocolate into the little stainless steel cup, and handed it to her. "It's still pretty hot."

Janet took a sip, then another. "Mmm. I love chocolate."

Jack grinned. "I never met a female of the human variety who didn't."

They stayed a while longer, sharing the hot chocolate and talking about Colorado's mountains, about the ranch, about their families.

Janet could get used to this. She could get used to being drenched in the natural beauty of the Cimarron. She could get used to spending time with this rough man who was always surprising her with his humor, his sensuality, his thoughtfulness. She could get used to waking up beside him in the morning, sharing the day with him, and lying beside him at night.

"What day is it?"

"Thursday," he answered.

On Saturday—Sunday at the latest—she'd have to head back to Denver to face the real world. She needed to get ready to start her new job on Monday. Of course, that didn't mean she couldn't come back.

"I'd like to come here again," she said.

"I'm happy to hear that." Jack took her gloved hand in his. "I want to share this with you, Janet. So, fair warning—I'm going to work hard to convince you that the Cimarron is now your home."

Janet wasn't sure she needed much more convincing.

"**D**o you know what we're going to do now?" Jack sat with his back against the edge of the tub, lazily fondling one of Janet's breasts, empty wine glasses sitting among the candles in the corner, the water growing cool.

"Get out of the tub?"

It had been late afternoon by the time they'd gotten back to the house. They'd rubbed down Buckwheat together and settled him in his stall. Then Jack had seen to Chinook before making dinner.

He chuckled. "We're going to have dessert—or I should have said *I'm* going to have dessert."

"What about me?"

"You *are* dessert."

Laughing, she turned in his arms. "What?"

Jack had been waiting for this moment. "I told you I wanted to taste you, and I wasn't kidding."

He let the water start draining from the tub, stood, and helped Janet to her feet. Then he climbed out of the tub and, ignoring her shriek of surprise, scooped her, slippery and wet, into his arms. "God, I love staring at your naked body. I'll take it up as a new hobby if you'll let me."

She laughed. "We might be able to work something out."

He positioned her on the edge of the bed, pillows beneath her hips, her legs resting over his shoulders. "Now I can see all of you, touch all of you, taste all of you."

He inhaled her sweet, musky fragrance, arousal shearing through him. It had been an eternity since he'd savored the scent of a woman.

"You don't have to do this." Her green eyes held uncertainty.

Did she feel self-conscious being open to him like this?

He would put an end to that right now.

"I *want* to do this." He teased her inner thighs with his fingertips, kissed and licked that delicate skin, hoping to help her relax. "I wish you could see how beautiful you are to me."

"You're not just saying that?"

He answered with a long, slow stroke of his tongue, tasting her from her vagina to her clitoris. Sure enough, that ended the discussion. She gasped, her thighs tensing, her fingers sliding into his hair.

He let himself explore her, drawing her inner lips into his mouth, stroking her clitoris with his tongue, teasing the entrance to her vagina. He went slowly, testing her, discovering what pleased her most, learning to read her sexual responses. Then he drew her clit into his mouth and sucked.

"Oh!" She gasped, her hips bucking off the bed, her fingers clenched tightly in his hair, her clit swelling as he sucked it, tugged on it with his lips, flicked it with his tongue.

God, she tasted good—wild and musky and sweet. He could have gone down on her forever. It didn't matter to him that his knees had begun to protest or that his dick was hard as granite or that his balls were on the brink of exploding. He wanted to give her every bit of pleasure she could take.

Remembering how sensitive her breasts were, he reached with one hand to palm her nipples, felt her petal-soft areolas pucker beneath his touch.

Her breathing was ragged now, her soft moans blatantly sexual, her fingers digging almost painfully into his hair.

He slid a finger inside her, then two, stroking her where she was most sensitive, her vagina slick and hot and tight. He felt those inner muscles tighten and knew she was close to the edge. He sucked a little harder, kept his rhythm steady. Her cries grew more frantic, every muscle in her body now tense.

Her breath caught and held, her body going stiff as the first tremors of climax washed through her. She exhaled in a shuddering cry, coming against his mouth, her body shaking. He stayed with her, kept his rhythm steady, the moisture of her orgasm drenching his fingers, lips, and tongue.

God, he loved her.

He hadn't been looking for her. He hadn't planned this. He hadn't imagined that he'd ever love another woman again. But he did.

Breathless, she scooted back onto the bed, reached for him. "Fuck me."

If he'd spoken that way to Theresa, even during sex, she'd have threatened to wash his mouth out with soap. Jack had been surprised when Janet had used these same words this morning. Now, her words sent a jagged bolt of lust blazing through him.

"Yes, ma'am." Hard to the point of aching, Jack rose, stretched out on the bed, drew her beneath him, and settled himself between her thighs, taking time to tuck a pillow beneath her left knee.

She took his hands in hers, stretched her arms over her head, then released his fingers, leaving him holding her wrists. And he got it.

She wanted him to pin her arms above her head.

So his Janet liked a little domination.

Well, wasn't that just perfect?

Jack had always had to curb that urge in himself for Theresa's sake. Now, he let himself go, tightening his grip on her wrists, pinning her hard against her pillow, letting her feel his strength.

She gave a little sigh of satisfaction, wiggling beneath him, her nipples puckering, her legs spreading wider.

He entered her with a single, slow thrust, stopping when she winced, then sliding deeper when he felt her muscles relax. She was slippery wet from her orgasm and as tight as a fist, and he found himself fighting to hold on. But he wanted to give her time, wanted her to enjoy this, too.

He willed himself to focus on her, on the physical act of making love to her, holding himself still inside her and grinding his pubic bone against hers. Her beautiful eyes were closed now, her lips parted, her body arching beneath his as the pleasure began to build for her once more. This time when she came, he went with her, the two of them soaring into oblivion together, lost in each other and the hot rush of orgasm.

CHAPTER TWELVE

J anet brushed Chipeta down, the docile mare watching her with a soft, dark eye. Jack was tied up on the phone in his office speaking with his attorney and bank, trying to arrange to put money in Kip's jail account, so she'd decided to make herself useful and had come out to the stables on her own to exercise the mares. One by one, she'd taken them out of their stalls, walked them to the riding barn, and let them run.

Baby Doe, Isabella Bird, and the feisty yearling Clara Brown had seized their moment of freedom, loping and galloping around the barn, then walking over to her when they'd had their fill. Molly Brown and Chipeta had been a little on the lazy side. They'd needed some urging with the wave of a lunge whip.

Not only had Janet enjoyed spending time with the horses, but she'd been pleased that she'd managed to exercise the five mares by herself. She was excited for Jack to find out what she'd done. He would understand what it meant to her.

God, it was going to be hard to leave the Cimarron. She knew she could come back on the weekends and find a warm welcome anytime. Jack had made that abundantly clear. But the idea of heading back to the hustle of Denver so that she could sit in meetings and occupy a desk now held absolutely no appeal to her. Still, she couldn't walk away from her career. She'd fought so hard to get where she was.

You're not where you were—not now, not anymore.

Last week, that realization would have left her feeling desolate. But now...

I've been thinking life just might have a few surprises left for me.

Life apparently held some surprises for her, too.

If someone had told her nine months ago that she'd have the best sex of her life with Jack West, she'd have thought they were insane, but it was true. He was an incredible lover, attentive and unselfish. She had no doubt that the two of them were sexually compatible in the long run. He read her cues the way he read the motions of a horse he was riding. She'd never experienced that kind of thoughtfulness from a man before, that depth of connection.

Was he in love with her? Did he hope to marry her one day?

He'd hinted that he might, but he hadn't come right out and said so. She didn't want to read too much into his words. But it didn't hurt to dream a little. When she'd been watching the mares lope and stomp around the riding barn, she'd spent more than a few minutes fantasizing about what it would be like to be Jack's wife, to share meals with him, to go to bed with him every night, to make the Cimarron her home.

She'd liked the way it made her feel. But after twenty years, could she just turn in her badge, collect her pension, and walk away?

"Are you really an FBI agent?"

Janet nearly jumped out of her skin. "Luke! I didn't hear you come in."

The young man blushed, shrugged. "Sorry."

"Yes, I am." She was—for the moment, anyway. "Are you really a cowboy?"

He grinned, adjusted the hat on his head. "I guess I am."

"How's your arm?"

He reached over, rubbed it. "It's healing. Still hurts some, though."

"I'll bet."

"Did the boss send you out here to tend the mares, because I told him I can handle it with Mr. Nate away, even with my arm."

"No, he didn't. He's busy, so I thought I'd make myself useful."

"And it's about damned time." Jack came around the corner, walked over to her, kissed her on the cheek. "I can't have you eating me out of house and home and doing nothing all day."

"I've exercised Chipeta, Baby Doe, Isabella Bird, and Molly and Clara Brown, and I did it by myself."

Jack's handsome face split in a broad grin, his gaze warm. "Did you now?"

"How did it go on your end?"

"I transferred a hundred dollars into Kip's commissary account via his attorney. It's not much, but it will make life a little more bearable. He's going to be behind bars for a very long time."

She smiled. "I admire your compassion."

"You're giving him money after what he did to me and Chinook?" Luke asked.

Janet had forgotten he was standing there.

"Have you ever been in jail, son? It's not an easy time. I'm doing for him what I hope someone would do for me in his shoes. I'd do it for you, too."

Luke looked at his feet.

"I'm glad you're here. I just got a call from Detective Sergeant Taylor. He said he has more questions for you and asked if he could come by this afternoon. He'll be at the house by one, so meet us there. In the meantime, check in with Chuck. I'm sending a group of men to shovel out Ms. Killeen's vehicle and tow it here. If you're up to it, I'm sure they could use your help."

"Yes, boss." Luke turned and walked away.

"He doesn't seem happy."

"He doesn't like doing anything that doesn't involve the horses. I told him when I hired him that he needed to be willing to do whatever job needed doing, but he seems to have forgotten that part."

"He's very young." Janet finished brushing down Chipeta, unhooked her cross ties, and led her toward her stall.

"Hell, they all seem young to me."

"Oh, stop! You've got more going on than any man in his twenties."

"Is that right?" He waited while she led Chipeta into her stall, then closed the stall door when the mare was safely inside. "What do you say that you and I go inside? I'd like to spend the next hour or so taking full advantage of the fact that I'm a man and you're a woman."

Janet looked into his eyes, felt that hitch in her chest again.

Oh, God!

She *was* in love with him.

J ack was in the middle of a conversation with Taylor when a knock came at his office door. "Come in."

It wasn't Luke who appeared, but Janet.

Jack motioned her toward a seat on the black leather sofa beside him. "Ms. Killeen has twenty years' experience with the FBI. Do you mind if she joins us?"

"I don't mind at all. I'd appreciate your perspective, SA Killeen." Det. Sgt. Taylor sat across from Jack wearing khaki uniform trousers and a dark brown fleece pullover with a star-shaped patch that read "Forest County Sheriff's Office" in place of a badge.

She handed him some pages from a notepad. "I asked Luke a few questions just after he was shot. These are my notes. Old habits die hard, I guess."

"Thanks." Taylor took her notes, glanced through them, his brow furrowed with concentration.

Jack turned to her. "He was just telling me that the Kimber they found in Kip's possession had a different serial number and was a different model than the one that was reported stolen."

Taylor looked up from Janet's notes. "That doesn't mean anything when it comes to confirming or disproving his guilt. We don't know that the stolen Kimber played any role in the shootings. Kip could have used any one of the forty-fives he owns. We won't know until the ballistics come back."

"I offered to expedite that," Janet said. "I'd be happy to get the evidence transferred to the Bureau and have it processed through us. You'd have it back in a matter of weeks."

Taylor gave her a sympathetic smile. "I'm not the one you need to convince."

Jack couldn't understand what Rove's problem was. "It seems to me we ought to have proof positive that Kip fired those shots before we condemn him to years in prison."

"A living eye witness is direct evidence," Taylor said. "You said Kip and Luke never met. The fact that Luke identified Kip from a lineup will seem pretty powerful to a jury. Combine that with motive and opportunity, and it's clear why the DA is pushing Kip to plead guilty. He believes he can avoid the expense of a trial."

"Do you mind if I look through your file?" Janet asked.

Taylor pushed the folder across the table toward her. "Go ahead."

Jack watched as she glanced quickly through the file, looking at photos of Chinook's wound, Luke's bleeding shoulder, the crime scene. He could see the wheels of her sharp mind turning. Although he appreciated her desire to help and knew that she was doing this partly out of concern for him, he didn't want her to have nightmares again.

Taylor turned to Jack. "Besides Kip Henderson, are there any other current or former employees who might feel they have a score to settle with you?"

Jack shook his head. "Hell, I don't know. I suppose there could be, but nothing comes to mind. I haven't gotten any threats."

"Is there anyone here at the ranch who might have a grudge against Kip?"

The question took Jack by surprise. He gave the answer some thought.

"He did win some pretty big money off a few of the men in a string of poker games. A couple of the men—Burt, Liam, and Joe—accused him of cheating, and some pretty strong words were exchanged. But no one threatened him, and no one got hurt. I put an end to it."

They were interrupted by a knock at the door.

"You wanted to see me?" Luke stepped in, cowboy hat in his hands. The powder burns on his face and neck were healing and almost matched his freckles now.

Janet closed the file and handed it back to Taylor.

Taylor stood, shook Luke's hand. "How's the arm?"

"It's better, I guess."

"I just wanted to fill in a few blanks and make certain I have the whole picture."

"Have a seat, son." Jack gestured to the other wingback chair.

Taylor waited for him to sit, opened his notes. "So, when the door opened, were you asleep or awake?"

"I'd been asleep, but I woke up right away."

"Did Kip leave the door open behind him, or did he close it?"

"I don't really remember. I think he left it open."

"Were the lights on or off?"

Luke seemed to consider it. "They were off because it was night and I was trying to sleep, but he turned them on. I guess he needed to see to shoot."

"Did he tell you who he was, or did you ask?"

"I asked who he was and what he was doing there."

"Did he try to shoot the stallion? Did he point his weapon that direction?"

Luke shook his head. "I think he saw me going for my gun."

"So you reached for your weapon before he fired?"

"Yeah, I did. I saw the gun in his hand. I had to defend myself and Chinook."

"Where was your weapon?"

"I had it with me under my pillow—just in case."

"How far away from you was he standing when he pulled the trigger?"

Luke looked angry, flustered. "Why do you keep asking me the same things I already answered?"

"Don't let it upset you," Jack reassured him. "It's standard procedure."

Luke nodded, grew calmer. "I don't remember. Close. It happened so fast."

"How many shots did you fire?"

"Two, I think. I really can't remember."

Taylor nodded, wrote that down. "How close was he when you fired?"

"Not far at all. I can't believe I missed."

"Adrenaline will screw up your aim like nothing else," Jack said.

Taylor pressed on. "Had he turned to go, or was he facing you when you fired?"

Luke shrugged. "I don't remember."

Taylor closed his notebook. "I think I've got everything I need."

"Can I go now?"

Taylor nodded to Jack.

"Yes, you may." Jack got to his feet, walked Luke to the door. "Thank you for your help, son."

"Luke, one last thing." This time it was Janet who asked the question. "Can you describe the weapon Kip was holding or tell us anything about it?"

Luke nodded. "It was a semi-auto with a fancy camo pattern on the grips."

Custom camo grips.

Janet gave him a warm smile. "Thanks, Luke."

"**W**hat's on your mind, angel? You've been a million miles away all evening."

Janet said what she was thinking. "Something about this just doesn't feel right."

"What do you mean?"

"I don't know. Call it a hunch. The way the case came together—it's too perfect, too … textbook. I know Taylor feels the same way. That's why he was here this afternoon. That's why he asked you those questions."

"You're saying you think Kip is innocent?"

She shrugged. "No. I don't know. Maybe."

"What brought this on?"

She wasn't sure how to quantify or explain her gut feeling. "I looked through the photos in Taylor's file. I was thinking how lucky we were that Kip didn't hit his target. Both times, he grazed his intended victim, then ran off and disappeared, even though he was standing no more than a few feet away."

Jack could understand this. "He was probably drunk and ratcheted up on adrenaline. I once watched a soldier unload his pistol at a VC at almost point-blank range. Seven shots—and not one of them hit the guy. He had to run the bastard through with his bayonet."

She knew how adrenaline worked. "That's not what I meant. Why, after coming all the way up here in the bad weather, did he fire only once each time? Why not keep firing until he accomplished his goal? He was standing right there. It's like he was afraid he might succeed. You say Kip was a crack shot?"

Jack nodded. "When he was sober."

"If he was so drunk he could barely hit the broadside of your barn, how did he manage to drive all the way up here, sneak onto your property, shoot like a drunk, then escape and get back to Denver without being seen or ending up in a car accident?"

Jack frowned. "I suppose stranger things have happened."

But Janet was just getting warmed up. "Here's another thing. Luke can't remember a host of details, but he does remember that the weapon Kip aimed at him had custom camo grips like the weapon the hunters reported stolen, even though the grips would have largely been concealed in Kip's hand."

"You think he's lying?"

"I think there's more to this than we know." She got to her feet. "Let's go to the stables. I want to do a walk-through."

"This is really important to you, isn't it?"

She looked into his eyes, saw that he was worried about her. "Yes, it is."

"Then it's important to me, too. I'll meet you in the mudroom in five."

She got to her feet, the facts of the case running through her mind, the images in the crime scene photos like a slideshow in her brain. She put on her boots, slipped into her parka, and was sliding her hands into her gloves when Jack appeared wearing his Colt in a shoulder holster, sat phone in his hand.

He tucked the phone into the pocket of his coat. "If there's any chance that the shooter is still out there..."

He didn't need to explain further.

They stepped out into the cold, and Janet stopped in her tracks. For a moment, all she could do was stare. "Look at the sky. God, that's beautiful."

The sun had long since set, and the sky was clear, a million stars glittering like diamonds. She could even see the Milky Way.

Jack chuckled, gave her hand a squeeze. "It's a good thing every now and again to look up at the sky."

She let herself look for a few more seconds, then moved on. "Let's pretend we're the shooter. Let's enter there."

"Whatever you say, SA Killeen." There was a teasing tone to his voice. "We need to go around to the other side."

They reached the door, which was both locked and cordoned off with yellow crime-scene tape.

"Are you trying to get me arrested?" He tore through the tape, then took out a ring of keys, unlocked the bolt, and slid the door open.

Inside, the stables were almost pitch black.

"How could anyone even see to find the light switch?"

"Kip knows where it is." As if to prove the point, Jack walked inside and flicked on the lights.

The switch was on the south wall next to Chinook's stall.

"So the shooter had to step in, walk a few feet inside in the dark, and flip the lights on." She followed in Jack's footsteps, processing this in her mind. "That puts him out of sight of Luke and his cot for a moment, doesn't it?"

Thanks to the walls of Chinook's stall, the shooter couldn't see Luke from this position, and Luke couldn't see the shooter.

But Kip would have been able to see the stallion.

"Why didn't he just shoot Chinook from here? He couldn't have known Luke was there until he stepped around the corner."

"Luke probably gave himself away when he challenged Kip."

"That could be." Janet moved on, filing all of this away. "According to Luke, the shooter stepped through the door, flipped on the lights. Luke woke up, asked him who he was, and he answered, 'Kip.'"

"Not very bright of him," Jack said.

Janet couldn't help but laugh. "Most criminals aren't all that smart."

She followed what she assumed had been the shooter's footsteps and walked out toward the center of the room. Luke's cot was still sitting where it had been that night. She walked to the place Luke said the shooter had stood. "Luke said the shooter came close to him, weapon drawn, saw him go for his gun and then shot him."

She stood there, looked down at the cot, thought of the many photos she'd seen—Luke's shoulder wound, the stippling on his skin. "Where did they find the slug?"

Jack walked toward the eastern wall, pointed to a white chalk circle at about chest height. "It's right here."

Janet held up her hands as if she had a gun and sighted on an imaginary Luke, her gaze shifting from where Luke had sat to the hole in the wall.

Chills ran down her spine.

"This doesn't make sense."

"What do you mean?"

"If Kip was standing and Luke was sitting on the cot, the bullet would have had a downward trajectory. Instead, it's lodged four feet off the ground. That round ought to have ended up somewhere closer to the floor."

Jack frowned, looked from the cot to the wall. "You're right. It doesn't line up."

"Also, Luke was shot in his right shoulder. That slug is to your left when it ought to be farther to your right. Whoever pulled the trigger had to be lower to the ground."

Or sitting on the cot.

CHAPTER THIRTEEN

"You're saying Luke shot himself?" Jack wanted to respect Janet's opinion, but this seemed completely off the deep end. "Why on God's green earth would he do that?"

"I don't know." Janet glanced around, as if the answers could be found somewhere in the scattered straw. "Maybe he wanted to cover for himself, put the blame on someone else for Chinook's shooting."

"Why would he shoot Chinook? The kid loves horses."

She seemed to consider this. "You said he doesn't like doing anything that doesn't involve the horses. He's gotten a lot of attention and praise from you and the other men since the night Chinook was shot. Maybe he was trying to prove himself. He created a crisis, then he helped you resolve it. He was even wounded."

Jack wasn't convinced. "He'd have to be awfully damned cool-headed. The smallest error, and he'd have broken Chinook's leg or killed himself."

But Janet wasn't listening. "Where's the weapon? He wouldn't have had time to run and hide it somewhere else before the other men responded to the gunfire. He was bleeding pretty heavily, and that would have left a trail. That means he must have hidden it somewhere in here."

"The sheriff's investigators turned this place inside out."

"You looking for this?"

Jack heard Luke's voice, heard Janet gasp, and stepped forward to see Luke standing just inside the doorway, a bag of oats spilled at his feet, a Kimber 1911 with what looked like camo grips in his hand, its barrel pointed at Janet.

Before Jack could clear his weapon, Luke had her, his arm around her neck, her body shielding his, the Kimber pressed against her temple. "I guess the sheriff's men didn't think to look through Chinook's feed."

Janet met Jack's gaze, and he saw determination in her eyes, not fear.

"Toss your piece over here." Luke's gaze was on Jack's Colt. "Nice and easy."

Jack kept his aim steady, sighting on Luke's forehead. "If you think I'm going to hand over my weapon just because you're pointing a gun at Ms. Killeen, you've been watching too much television."

Luke glared at him. "You don't understand. All I have to do is pull this trigger—"

"Harm the woman I love, and there will be no escape for you anywhere on this earth. Do you understand me?" Jack waited for an answer, then repeated his question, this time shouting. "*Do you understand me?*"

Luke jumped, but didn't lower the pistol. "It didn't have to be like this, you know. You were starting to trust me, and then she had to get involved."

Jack couldn't believe what he was hearing. "You shot Chinook, my champion stallion, to make me trust you?"

Goddamn.

Janet had been right.

"I wanted you to see how good I was with horses so you'd let me take care of Chinook and the mares on my own instead of making me work with that scar-faced son of yours. But instead of asking for my help, you made me shovel snow and do all kinds of meaningless shit. You even sent me off to make coffee like I was a woman or something. So I came up with a better way to impress you."

There was no doubt in Jack's mind now.

Luke was a sociopath.

Fear spread like ice through Jack's veins. "You shot yourself to make it look like you'd risked your life defending Chinook."

"It took a lot of guts, you have to admit. If I didn't aim exactly right, I'd blow my own head off or shoot myself through the heart."

"Well, I'm impressed with your marksmanship, but you're a gutless coward. You're holding a gun to the head of an unarmed woman, hiding behind her."

"She's not a woman, not really. She's a fed." Luke spat those last words with contempt. "If I let her go, you'll just shoot me."

"Why don't I give you the keys to one of my trucks? I'll toss them over to you, and you can take whichever truck you like and go anywhere." Jack took one hand off his pistol and reached into his coat pocket, his gaze never leaving Luke's.

Luke waved his weapon at Jack. "No! Get your hands out of your pocket!"

But Jack had already dialed out on his sat phone. He didn't remember whom he'd spoken to last, but that person was about to get a strange call. He hoped whoever it was would listen long enough to realize what was happening. He slowly withdrew his hand from his pocket, his keys in hand. "What's the problem? You getting jumpy, son?"

"You'll toss those keys over, and the moment I reach for them, you'll shoot me."

Jack tossed the keys onto the cot. "I'm not going to do that, but I'm glad you're thinking about your situation. You're in a world of trouble. We know the truth. Detective Sergeant Taylor is on to you, too. How do you think this is going to end? Do you think killing us will make your troubles disappear? It won't."

"Listen to him, Luke," Janet said. "Right now, you're only looking at animal abuse and false reporting. You might even get probation. If you kill us, you—"

"Shut up!" Luke tightened his grip on Janet, choking her.

Damn it!

"You are one crazy son of a bitch if you think being rough with her is going to improve your situation. If you want to get out of this in one piece, you'd best let her go. And I mean now."

Luke's face turned red, and he took a step toward Jack, dragging Janet with him. "You don't give me orders anymore, old man."

Janet's leg couldn't support the sudden movement, and she slipped, leaving Luke exposed from the waist down.

It had been more than forty years since Jack had shot a man, but when he saw his chance he took it.

BAM! BAM!

Luke dropped the pistol, releasing Janet as he collapsed to the ground, shrieking in pain, hands pressed against his right thigh.

Janet fell forward, grabbed for the Kimber. But Luke lunged for it, too, throwing himself on top of her, slamming his fist into her face, the two of them struggling for it out of Jack's view on the other side of the cot.

He rushed in, weapon raised.

BAM!

A shot rang out, but it wasn't Jack who'd pulled the trigger.

His heart seemed to explode. "Janet!"

Luke sat bolt upright, grinned at Jack, a strange expression on his face.

Agony exploded in Jack's chest, his heart shattering.

Janet!

His finger tightened on the trigger, black rage driving him. "You son of a bitch!"

Then blood bubbled up from Luke's mouth, and he toppled sideways, a hole shot clean through his chest.

"Janet?" On a surge of relief, Jack closed the distance, grabbed the bastard's coat, and dragged his body off her.

Janet lay on her back, pistol in both hands, blood on her cheek, a stunned expression on her face. "Oh, Jack!"

Jack took the pistol from her, drew her into his arms. "Jesus, are you okay?"

Chuck appeared in the doorway, sat phone in his hand. "Holy shit!"

"Call nine-one-one. We need an ambulance and the sheriff out here. Luke just tried to kill the two of us. Janet's been injured."

She shook her head. "I'm fine, really."

"Like hell you are." He caught her chin, tilted her head so that he could see. "He split your cheek."

She drew back. "We should check him ... maybe do first aid."

"He's dead." Jack gathered her in his arms. "Would you please just let me hold you? God, woman! For a moment there, I thought I'd lost you."

Her arms went around him. "I thought you'd lost me, too."

And for a time they held each other, barely aware of the men who gathered at the stable door.

The next several hours passed in a blur of questions—questions from detectives, questions from paramedics, questions from hospital staff. Images from the night ran through her mind. Jack pointing his Colt at Luke, cold fury on his face. Luke's surprise when she'd shot him. His corpse lying in a pool of blood on the straw-covered concrete.

It was sometime after midnight when she finally found herself alone with Jack in one of the ER bays. "Have you ever killed anyone?"

He nodded. "Yes, though I couldn't say for sure how many. It was a long time ago, and I didn't keep count."

Vietnam. Of course. How could she have been so stupid?

"I'm sorry. That was a thoughtless question."

He gave her hand a squeeze. "How about you?"

She shook her head. "Not till tonight."

She had taken a life. She didn't regret it. If Luke had gotten his hands on that pistol, he'd have killed her and Jack without a second thought.

"I'm so sorry." Jack watched her through troubled eyes. "I'm so sorry this happened. I should have brought you back to Denver the moment the highway reopened."

Janet ought to have realized he'd torture himself. "Stop! How could you have known this was going to happen? Besides, I helped, didn't I?"

"Yes, you certainly did. You figured it out before any of them."

"Taylor knew." Janet was sure of it. "He was just trying to put all the pieces together before making an accusation that might end his career."

"You'll learn to live with having killed," Jack said.

It bothered her that she felt so troubled by it. "I don't regret it."

"Of course you don't, but it gnaws at you just the same."

"Yes." That's exactly how it was.

Jack raised her hand to his lips, kissed it. "When that shot went off and Luke sat up, there was a split second when I thought he'd gotten the gun and you were … " He closed his eyes, his anguish putting a lump in her throat. "I don't know what I would have done if he'd killed you, Janet. You mean more to me than—"

The doctor walked in, interrupting them. "It looks like your MRI results are normal. Let's get that laceration cleaned up, and we'll send you home. I'd like you to stay with someone tonight. They'll need to keep an eye on you and make sure you're not showing signs of head trauma."

"I'll be with her," Jack said.

His words, full of confidence and affection, helped melt away some of the darkness that had wrapped itself around her heart. Yes, she had taken a life, but because of that, she and Jack were still here, free to live theirs.

By the time her discharge papers were ready and Jack had paid her insurance co-pay—he'd insisted—it was early in the morning, and all she wanted was to sleep.

"Take me home, Jack."

He nodded. "Do you want to stop by the ranch to get your things, or do you want to head straight to Denver?"

As tired as she was, she smiled. "Take me home—to the ranch."

He grinned. "Yes, ma'am."

She fell asleep in the truck, and he had to wake her. He helped her inside, brought her water and a pain pill. She accepted it gratefully, undressing while he lit a fire in the fireplace. Then she sank into bed.

He tucked the duvet under her chin. "Sleep, angel."

"You're coming to bed, too, aren't you?"

"In a minute. I just want to make sure everything is locked up tight."

She was asleep before he returned. When nightmares woke her, as she'd feared they might, he was right there to hold her and to banish those dreams to the darkness.

J ack had known Nate would be pissed off. He'd just gotten off the phone with Kip, who'd been released from jail this morning, all charges dropped, when Nate cornered him in his office and shut the door.

"What the hell were you thinking? Luke gets shot, and I don't hear a damned thing about it? You should have called me. I'd have left Megan and Emily in Denver and come up here to help out. Javier would have come with me. Luke wouldn't have tried this shit with the two of us around."

Nate had read the email Jack had sent him last night and had headed up the canyon with Megan and Emily at the crack of dawn.

"Things seemed under control, and I felt you had enough to worry about with a child and a pregnant wife in law school."

"Dad, we're talking about bullets here! The two of you could have been shot or killed. When the heat is on, my place is here at the ranch by your side."

"You're right, son. I should have called you. I apologize."

"How could this have happened? I thought Luke came with a glowing recommendation from one of Chuck's buddies."

"Taylor checked into that. It seems Chuck's friend gave him a recommendation in hopes of getting rid of Luke. Some of the men felt uncomfortable around him, and one of their mares had some unexplained injuries."

"So they dumped their personnel problem on us."

"Seems like." It had infuriated Jack when he'd heard this news.

"Why did Luke blame Kip, and how in the hell did he ID Kip in a lineup when he'd never seen the man?"

"Turns out he did see him for just a few minutes when he went into town with Chuck for supplies. Chuck stopped at Kip's place to pick up his key to the bunkhouse. Luke didn't meet him, but we figure he caught a glimpse of Kip when he opened his door."

"Ah, well, that explains that. But let's talk about *why* you didn't call me."

"Haven't we already gone over that?"

"You wanted time alone with Janet." It was a statement, not a question.

Jack saw no point in denying his feelings. "I love her. One day, I hope to convince her that the Cimarron is her home."

Nate's eyebrows rose. "You want to *marry* her?"

"Now that you mention it, yes, I do."

"What does she think of this?"

"Well, I don't know. I haven't asked her yet."

"Isn't this kind of sudden?"

"When you get to be my age, son, you don't have a lot of time for bullshit. I can't explain it. She and I just clicked. How long were you and Megan together before you knew you were in love with her?"

Nate opened his mouth, shut it, looked at the floor.

"Exactly."

Some of the anger left Nate's face. "You really care about her."

"Yeah, I do. I never thought I'd feel this way about a woman again. I didn't go looking for this, but it happened. I know it must be hard for you to think about another woman being in the house."

Nate shook his head. "You're wrong about that. Mom would want you to be happy. That's what I want, too."

"No one will ever replace your mother, but my heart seems to be big enough to love two women in this lifetime. I consider that a blessing."

Nate smiled. "So do I."

"I hope you'll make her feel welcome. She's a special woman. She's had a terrible hard time of it since getting shot. Being here with me, riding horses again, working in the stables—it's been good for her. It's helped her recapture a part of her life she thought she'd lost. If anyone ought to understand that, son, it's you."

Nate nodded. "When do I get to meet her?"

Janet recognized Nate the moment she walked into the kitchen. "I'm so happy finally to meet you. You look so much like your father."

Nate smiled. "We almost met last time you were here. I was just driving up when the old man tossed you off the property."

"Why do you have to remind her of that?" Jack, who was busy stirring pancake batter, glowered at his son.

Nate introduced her to Megan, who was tall and willowy, with brilliant green eyes and long auburn hair pulled back in a ponytail. She sat at the table looking miserable, a cup of tea and a few crackers sitting on a plate in front of her.

"Morning sickness?" Janet asked.

Thank God she'd never have to deal with that at least.

Megan nodded. "They say it's a sign of a healthy pregnancy, but it sure doesn't feel that way."

Nate reached out, touched Megan's shoulder, offering her silent support.

Then a little girl with blond hair and bright blue eyes bounded into the kitchen. She eyed Janet. "Are you Grandpa Jack's girlfriend?"

Unsure how Jack would want her to answer, Janet changed the subject. "You must be Emily. Your grandpa has told me so much about you."

Emily gave her a shy smile. "You're pretty."

"Thank you." Janet didn't know why the child's words touched her, but they did.

"I'm going to be a big sister," Emily said. "My daddy breeded my mommy, like Chinook with the mares."

Megan coughed, choking on her tea.

Jack looked over at Nate. "What the hell did you tell this child?"

Nate shrugged. "It's not what we said. It's what she put together. She does live on a stud farm, you know."

Janet fought not to laugh. "Congratulations! You must be so excited."

But Emily's fleet little mind had moved on. "Grandpa Jack is making chocolate chip flapjacks. He only makes those for Sunday breakfast, but we weren't here last Sunday, so I said he should make them two days in a row. Right, Grandpa Jack?"

"Right, Miss Emily." Jack stirred a cup of chips into the batter. "Now, skedaddle and wash your hands."

Emily darted from the room.

Janet touched her hand to Jack's arm. "She really does have you wrapped around her finger, doesn't she?"

Megan shook her head.

Nate rolled his eyes. "You have no idea."

But Jack only smiled, his gaze warm. "She's not the only one."

CHAPTER FOURTEEN

On Monday, Janet went to work at her new job. It seemed the sensible thing to do. She couldn't just turn her back on a 20-year career and leave the Agency to be with a man she'd known for only a week. Everything with Jack was so new.

It took her less than a month to realize that being sensible was stupid.

The job was every bit as boring as she'd feared it would be—meetings, meetings, and more meetings. Sitting at a desk forty hours a week was hard on her hip. But worse than that, she missed Jack, missed the mountains, missed the rhythm of daily life, the fresh air, the horses.

Already, the Cimarron felt like home. She'd left so many things at the ranch—toiletries, makeup, clothes—that she now had her own closet in Jack's bedroom. Nate and Megan, who were also in Denver during the work week while Megan finished her first semester of law school, had made her feel like part of the family, inviting her over for supper after work. Nate had even come to shovel her walk without being asked.

But Janet lived for the weekends when Jack would pick her up and drive her back to the Cimarron, where he spoiled her with good food, good conversation, and sex so amazing it blew her mind. She'd never had a lover like him.

She'd told him this one night when she'd lain beside him, sexually spent and replete, her body floating.

He'd drawn her into his arms, kissed her. "That's because no man has ever loved you the way I do."

She knew he wanted to ask her to marry him, knew he was giving her time to get used to her new job, her new routine, her new life. When Megan showed Janet her wedding ring and oh-so-casually asked what kind of ring she'd always wanted, Janet knew the day was drawing near.

But whatever plans he was making got put on hold when Janet learned she was being sent to Quantico to attend a week-long conference about intra-agency cooperation. She'd be leaving on a Sunday and getting back on a Saturday, which meant losing four whole nights with him.

"We'll make up for it when you get back," he said. "I promise."

Jack held Janet's hair while she threw up, then got her a cold washcloth.

She looked up at him, misery etched into her pretty face. "I'm so sorry."

"Why are you apologizing?"

"You made such a wonderful dinner, and I can't keep it down."

"Don't even think about that. It's not important."

Jack was worried. Janet had been sick ever since coming home from Quantico. At first, they thought she'd picked up the stomach flu at that damned conference. Now it seemed she'd come down with something more serious, some lingering food-related illness. He'd had big plans to surprise her with a proposal and an engagement ring, but had put all of that on hold until she was well.

"I want you to see the doctor tomorrow."

She nodded. "I'll call first thing in the morning and make an appointment."

"Let's get you to bed."

She nodded, reached for his hand.

He helped her to her feet, made sure she had her cane, then went to turn down the covers while she brushed her teeth.

She walked out of the bathroom, climbed into bed. "God, I feel hungry now."

"I don't think I'd trust your stomach if I were you." He pulled the duvet up to her chin. "I'll go make you some tea."

Downstairs, Nate was reading Emily a bedtime story. "How is she?"

"She lost her supper—again. She's going to see her doctor tomorrow." He walked into the kitchen to find Megan doing the dishes.

"I'm heating water for tea. It might help calm her stomach."

Jack gave Megan a pat on the shoulder. "You must have read my mind."

Now twelve weeks pregnant, Megan had had a rough go of it this past month, sick every morning and exhausted. She'd struggled to make it through her classes and get her studying done each night. So far, her professors had been understanding, and Nate had taken up much of the slack with Emily so that Megan could sleep and study.

"You go rest. I'll finish the dishes."

"Thanks." Megan shot him a smile. "I still have five chapters of reading to go."

"You'll get it done. I have faith in you."

By the time Jack had finished the dishes and wiped down the table, the tea kettle was whistling. He poured boiling water into a small porcelain teapot, added a bag of mint tea leaves, then put the teapot together with a mug and a small jar of honey on a tray and carried it to the bedroom, only to find Janet sound asleep.

He set the tray down on the nightstand, brushed a strand of hair off her cheek, and watched her sleep.

J anet sat on a chair in the exam room, hoping she wouldn't throw up on the floor and watching while Dr. Rivera, a kind young woman with dark shoulder-length hair, typed in Janet's symptoms—nonstop nausea, vomiting, dizziness, fatigue.

Dr. Rivera turned to her. "There are a variety of tests we can run, but first I'd like to do a thorough exam. Undress down to your underwear."

She gave Janet a gown, then left her alone to take off her sweater and leggings, returning a few minutes later with a nurse. She listened to Janet's lungs and her heart, looked in her throat and ears, then asked her to lie back and began poking around on her abdomen. "When was your last period?"

"It's been a year, I guess. Menopause hits the women of my family early."

"Have you had unprotected sex in the past few months?"

Janet stared at her. "You don't think…"

"I think you might be pregnant."

Janet's pulse spiked. She sat up, clutching the gown around her like a shield. "I don't understand how that could happen. I'm forty-five. I've been pre-menopausal for four years."

"I've had women get pregnant naturally who were older than you are. Unless a woman goes a full calendar year without a period, we don't consider her to be in menopause. You could go six or seven or even eleven months without a period and then suddenly ovulate."

Janet shook her head. "I just don't think it's possible."

"Slip out of your panties. I'd like to do a pelvic exam, if that's okay."

Janet took off her underwear, then lay back on the exam table and let Dr. Rivera put her feet in stirrups, wincing at the pain caused by the cold, hard speculum.

"Try to relax," Dr. Rivera said.

Right. Sure.

How was Janet supposed to do that?

"Your cervix is blue, a good indicator of pregnancy. I'm going to palpate your uterus." She was silent for a moment, her pushing and prodding causing Janet discomfort. "I'd definitely say you're pregnant. What you've been experiencing is hyperemesis gravidarum."

Janet covered her eyes with her hands. "I don't believe this."

"I take it this pregnancy is a surprise?"

Major understatement.

"You could say that."

"Do you have a relationship with the father?"

"Yes, but he certainly won't be expecting this."

No, he wouldn't. She'd told him she couldn't get pregnant.

Dr. Rivera kept a soothing hand on Janet's leg, turned to her nurse, and spoke quietly. "Go get me a Doppler."

Janet was helped to a sitting position, then given privacy to dress again. As she put on her clothes, she was so stunned she didn't know whether to laugh or cry, her motions automatic, her emotions and thoughts jumbled.

The doctor returned with a little device in her hands. "I'd like to listen for the baby's heartbeat, if that's okay."

This entire situation was surreal.

"Sure." Why not?

And maybe unicorns would fly through the room in the meantime.

Fighting hysterical laughter, Janet got back up on the table, lay back, and pushed her leggings down to her hips like Dr. Rivera asked.

"This will be a little cold." The doctor put some goo on the end of a small, wand-like probe, then pressed the probe against Janet's lower abdomen, moving it slowly, pressing it deeper, angling the head of it this way and that.

Squish. Squish. Squish. Squish.

"That's it. That's your baby's heartbeat. I'm guessing you're about nine weeks at this point. You'll need an ultrasound to be certain, given that we don't have a date of your last menstrual period."

Janet listened to the little sound, stunned to think a baby was growing inside her—Jack's baby. She hadn't planned on being a mother, and she knew Jack hadn't planned on being a father again. Was this really happening?

"I'm going to put a call in to a high-risk OB. Because of your age, your pelvic injuries, and because of your hyperemesis, you're going to need to see a high-risk doc. In the meantime, I'm admitting you to St. Anthony's. Your dizziness is due in part to dehydration and low electrolytes. You need rest and IV fluids and possibly medication."

The situation kept getting stranger.

"You want me to go to the hospital?"

"You can go home first, if you want, pack a few things together. Head to St. Anthony's, and go straight to admitting. I'll call in the admitting orders."

Dr. Rivera went on, explaining what hyperemesis gravidarum was and how it was treated, then telling Janet about some of the risks associated with pregnancy in older woman. Janet barely heard what she said, one thought running through her mind.

How was she going to tell Jack?

Jack grabbed his keys and headed straight to the garage, shouting over his shoulder to Nate. "She didn't say what was wrong, only that it wasn't serious. Her doctor wants to admit her for IV fluids and rest. She wants me to meet her at her place and drive her to the hospital."

Nate followed him. "Call as soon as you know anything."

Jack climbed into the cab of his truck, almost forgetting to raise the garage door before backing out and heading down the road toward the front gate, his mind holding on to one thought: She'd said it wasn't serious.

The drive to Denver seemed to take forever, traffic snarling the moment he hit that proverbial pain in the ass known as I-70. He called Janet twice along the way, just to hear her voice and make sure she was okay.

"I'm fine," she said. "Drive safely, okay?"

It took almost two hours to reach her house. It felt like an eternity. He parked, walked up the sidewalk, and knocked.

She opened the door, and he could see she'd been crying. She slipped into his arms, a troubled expression on her face. "We need to talk."

He sat on her sofa beside her, held her hand. "I'm listening."

"Jack... Oh, God." She buried her face in her hands for a moment, then looked into his eyes. "I've decided I'm going to quit my job, retire early."

"You're leaving the FBI?" What did this have to do with her being sick—unless she was really very ill?

"Yes ... because I'm pregnant."

Jack heard the thrum of his pulse against his ears. "You're ... what?" Had the floor just tilted beneath his feet?

She burst into tears, words tumbling out of her in a rush. "I know I told you I couldn't get pregnant, but somehow I did. I thought I was menopausal, but I guess I wasn't quite yet. The doctor said some women can still ovulate even when they haven't had a period for almost a year, so I guess that's what happened, but I swear this wasn't deliberate. I didn't try to trick you or—"

"Hey, come here." He drew her into his arms, held her. "So, you're pregnant."

She sniffed. "The doctor said I'm about nine weeks."

That meant she must have conceived that first week she'd stayed with him.

Well, I'll be damned.

Jack held back a surge of elation. Janet hadn't planned on having children, and given her injuries, he wasn't sure she could carry a baby safely to term. In the end, what happened next wasn't his choice to make, but hers.

"So all of your being sick has been morning sickness?" It certainly had lasted far beyond the morning.

"I have hyperemesis gravidarum—that's Latin for 'too much barfing,' I think. They want to give me IV fluids and see if I can't keep some food down."

He kissed her hair. "Whatever you decide to do, I'll stand by you."

She pulled back, looked up at him. "You're not angry?"

He shook his head. "Why on God's green earth would I be angry that the woman I love is pregnant with our baby?"

She gave him a tremulous smile, her cheeks wet with tears. "I want to have this baby—if I can. It's not going to be without risks, but I want to try. I know you weren't expecting this. Neither was I."

Jack couldn't help but smile, the elation he'd held back finally washing through him. "Out of all the surprises life has sent my way, this is one of the best."

She sank against him, wrapped her arms around him. "I was so worried you'd be upset or want me to get rid of it."

"Not in a million years."

They were going to have a baby together. He was going to be a father. At the age of 63, he was going to be a father again—if all went well.

"Let's get you to the hospital."

They checked in at St. Anthony's twenty minutes later. Jack pushed Janet in a wheelchair to a private room, where a nurse hooked her up to a couple of different IVs. In a matter of minutes, Janet was asleep, clearly exhausted.

Jack slipped out of the room and into the hallway and dialed Nate's number. How in the hell was he going to explain this?

Nate answered on the second ring. "Is she okay?"

"Yes, but… Well, son, she's pregnant."

Nate laughed. "Are you serious?"

"Yes, I'm serious. I'm not exactly sure how it happened, but—"

"Now, Dad, I thought we already had this talk." This was followed by more laughter. "I think you breeded Janet like Chinook—"

"Son, shut your mouth for a minute." When Jack was satisfied that Nate was listening, he went on. "Because of her age and her injuries, there are a fair number of risks. She's got hyperemesis gravi… hell, something that makes her throw up a lot, so they're giving her IV fluids and some drug to stop the nausea."

"Poor thing. I hope it helps. Is there any risk to her or the baby right now?"

"We have a lot of questions, but not many answers yet."

"God, I can't wait to tell Megan."

"See that you don't tell anyone else. I want to put a ring on her finger and walk her down the aisle before word of this gets out so that no one can accuse her of forcing me into marriage or say that I married her just because I got her pregnant."

For some reason, this made Nate laugh again. "A father at the age of sixty-four."

"I'm sixty-three."

"You won't be by the time the baby arrives."

"Shit." He hadn't thought of that.

"Seriously, congratulations, Dad. This baby is very lucky to have you as a father. Trust me on this. I know."

Jack's throat suddenly got tight. "Thanks, son."

Janet watched the screen, holding fast to Jack's hand while Dr. Fleming moved the ultrasound probe on her lower belly.

"There's your baby." The doctor pointed to the screen. "That's its little heart. This big part here is its head. That's a leg. It's moving."

Janet stared in amazement, barely able to speak. "It's really real."

Until this moment, some part of her expected the doctor to tell her there'd been a mistake and, oh, by the way, she actually had giardia instead.

But there it was in black and white—their baby.

She looked up at Jack to find him staring at the screen, a look of amazement on his face. He smiled down at her. "You bet it's real."

"It's too early to tell the sex, of course," Dr. Fleming said. "But you've decided you don't want to know, right?"

"We want to be surprised," Janet answered.

Not that they hadn't already had a few big surprises these past weeks.

"Let's see if we can get a measurement here." Dr. Fleming pushed some buttons on the machine. "You're measuring at nine and a half weeks pregnant. That puts your due date on or around June 23."

"That's right at the end of foaling season." Jack grinned, gave her hand a squeeze.

"We've got a strong heartbeat." Dr. Fleming turned on the audio.

The small, dark room filled with the rapid thrum of a tiny beating heart.

Tears blurred Janet's vision, spilled down her temples. "Do you hear that?"

Jack nodded, a soft smile on his face. "I surely do."

She wiped the tears from her cheeks. "I've still got so long to go. So much could go wrong. I don't know whether I should feel elated, cautiously optimistic, or scared to death right now."

Dr. Fleming laughed. "It sounds like you're well on your way to being a mother."

But Jack bent down, kissed her cheek. "Whenever life gives you the option, go with elation. That's what I'm feeling."

J ack drove Janet back to her place, helped her pack a few suitcases, and then piled them in the back of his truck and headed home. It was early evening by the time they reached the Cimarron. Jack drove by the main gate, kept heading up the highway.

"Hey, aren't we supposed to turn there?"

He gave Janet's hand a squeeze. "I've got something to show you."

He continued up the highway, most of the snow now melted, true autumn setting in up in the high country. He turned off onto the dirt road that led to the high pasture, not stopping for the cattle, which now grazed on meadow grass. Taking care to avoid ruts, he slowly drove up the road, then made a left onto the oldest road on the ranch, what was left of the original homestead house about fifty yards ahead of them.

He drove up to the house, stopped, parked. "I'll come and help you out."

He opened her door, helped her to the ground, kept his arm around her, wanting to make certain she didn't slip and fall. "Follow me."

"What is this place?" She looked around them, craning to see it all—the orchard, the old barn, the outhouse, the iron water pump.

"This is the house my grandfather built for my grandmother when he got the crazy idea to homestead in the Rocky Mountains."

Most of the place was still standing, though the paint had long since worn away, and the wood was in bad shape. The glass windows were still intact, tattered yellow curtains hanging in what had once been the sitting room. The chimney had crumbled a bit, remnants of a bird's nest showing at the top.

Jack slowly walked in a circle around the house, holding Janet's hand. "He came up here in 1927 with my pregnant grandmother and a two-year-old son, who, as it happens, was my father. He woke up one day and decided he couldn't do right by his family in the city. He'd fought in World War I—signed up when he turned eighteen and ended up at the Battle of the Argonne, saw most of his friends die. I think he needed to get away from the noise and find peace."

They stopped on the side of the house in full view of the surrounding mountains.

Jack watched the awe on Janet's face as she took in the view, the breeze catching her dark hair, the cold putting color back in her cheeks.

She closed her eyes, inhaled. "It is peaceful up here and so quiet. I can't even hear the highway."

It made him smile to see her reaction, to see how the land called to her. She belonged here now. She belonged with him. But did she know that?

He would find out in a moment.

"Why did they abandon this house?"

"My grandfather picked this spot for its beauty." He pointed to a dead Douglas fir that had been almost split in two by lightning, its bark blackened. "What he didn't know is that a load of iron ore runs right beneath it, making this stretch of land especially prone to lightning strikes."

She laughed. "I can see how that would be a problem."

"He ended up leaving this house and building another one lower down. Theresa and I had that one razed to its foundation and built the ranch house you see today."

Get to the damned point, amigo.

But Janet had a half-dozen other questions.

Were those apple trees? Did the well still have drinkable water? What had his grandparents done in the winter when the snow got deep? How long did it take them to get to Denver when they needed supplies—or did they go to Scarlet Springs? What if they had to go to the bathroom in the middle of the night? And, God, what had his grandmother done when she'd had morning sickness?

He answered as best he could, feeling more nervous by the minute.

"I brought you up here because I wanted you to see where it started. Whether you realize it or not, you've become a part of the Cimarron now, a part of its history. I wanted to do this a few weeks ago, before we found out you were pregnant. It's important to me that you understand that."

She looked up at him, confused. "You wanted to bring me here?"

"No, that's not what I meant."

Just get to it, damn it!

He reached into his pocket, took out the engagement ring he'd had made for her—a two-karat oval diamond set in platinum—then released her hand and got down on one knee. "I love you, Janet. I want to spend the rest of my life with you. No matter how many surprises the future brings, I want you at my side. Will you do me the honor of becoming my wife?"

Then he realized he hadn't opened the box.

Jesus Christ on a crutch! Had he bungled it like this with Theresa?

But she wasn't looking at the box. She was looking at him, tears in her eyes, a wobbly smile on her face. "You finally asked me! Please stand up so I can kiss you."

He got to his feet, and she jumped into his arms, kissing him right on the mouth, a deep, hungry kiss. "Is that a 'yes'?"

"Yes, Jack, I'll marry you." She laughed, the sound making his chest swell.

"Don't you even want to see the ring first?" He released her, opened the box, held it up for her to see.

Her eyes went wide. "Oh, my God! It's ... *beautiful*."

He took it from the box, slid it onto her ring finger. "I'd like to get married as soon as possible. I don't want anyone casting aspersions on your character or thinking I married you only because of a baby."

"You're so good to me." She wrapped her arms around him. "Sliding off the highway was the best thing that's ever happened to me."

"You didn't know it, angel, but you were coming home."

As they turned to walk back to the truck, the setting sun cleared the clouds, bathing the valley before them in gold.

EPILOGUE

June 15

"I'm scared." Janet looked up at Jack, the bright lights of the operating room and the beeping of the heart monitor adding to her anxiety.

Jack stroked her cheek, smiled down at her, a blue surgical cap on his head. "Take a deep breath and relax, angel. You've done your part. Let Dr. Fleming do his."

Janet hadn't wanted a C-section, but with age, the blood pressure problems that had popped up in her third trimester, and her pelvic injuries, Dr. Fleming had felt it would be safest both for her and the baby. She'd talked with him about preserving as many elements of natural birth as she could since this would be the only time in her life she would have this experience. But here in this moment, she just wanted it to be over.

"Can you feel this?" Dr. Fleming asked from the other side of a blue drape that blocked her view of the surgery.

"No." She couldn't feel anything, the epidural leaving her completely numb from the ribcage down, making her upper body seem strangely heavy.

"We're going to scrub down your skin, and then you should have your baby in just a few minutes."

Janet closed her eyes, tightened her grip on Jack's hand.

He leaned down, kissed her cheek. "It's going to be a boy."

That made her smile. Jack had been telling her since the beginning that the baby would be a boy. For four generations, his family had produced only boys—well, five generations if you counted Nate and Megan's baby boy, Jackson, who'd been named after his grandfather and was almost four weeks old now.

She opened her eyes, looked up at him. "Boy or girl—I'm happy either way."

"So you don't know what the baby is?" the anesthesiologist asked from behind her surgical mask.

"We're doing it the old-fashioned way," Jack answered.

"Do you want me to tell you what I'm doing?" Dr. Fleming asked.

Janet thought about it for a moment. "Yes, please."

"I'm making the first incision, cutting through the skin."

Janet squeezed her eyes shut at the thought, though she felt no pain.

"Easy, angel," Jack said, his grip on her hand firm.

"Do you have names picked out?" someone asked.

The room seemed to be filled with people, and Janet recognized none of them because their hair and faces were all hidden.

"No," The sound of Jack's voice was soothing, his free hand caressing her shoulder. "We thought we'd wait and see who this little person was before naming him."

"Or her," Janet added.

"It's going to be a boy."

"I'm making an incision into your abdominal cavity. I'm being extra careful here in case your previous surgery left any adhesions. In a moment, you'll feel some tugging and some pressure. I need to make certain the incision is large enough for your baby to get through."

Janet closed her eyes, drew deep breaths, the odd sensation of tugging deep in her belly strange and not entirely comfortable.

"Slow, deep breaths." Jack kissed her cheek.

He'd been so strong for her, coming to all of her appointments, massaging her hip day and night to help ease the pain caused by the weight of the baby, making meals that were not only nutritious but which also catered to her food cravings—and Megan's. He'd been so respectful of her wishes and responsive to her fears. He'd been her hero.

"Okay, we're getting down to business here. I'm cutting into your uterus."

"You'll have your baby in your arms in just a minute," a woman's voice said.

"I just broke your amniotic sac, and we're suctioning out the fluid," Dr. Fleming said. "I think this baby wants out. Its head is right here."

"Look at all that dark hair," one of the nurses said.

Janet met Jack's gaze. "Oh, my God. We're having a baby."

He smiled. "*You're* having a baby. In a minute, you're going to be a mother."

"Let's lower the drape so they can see," Dr. Fleming said.

The blue surgical drape was lowered, and Janet found herself staring at the surreal sight of her bulging belly. There wasn't as much blood as she'd expected, but there was some. And then Dr. Fleming's hand disappeared into her abdomen.

There was more pressure, more tugging, and one of the assistants pushed down on her abdomen.

Then Dr. Fleming's hand reappeared as he eased the baby's head from inside her. "The head is out."

Janet watched in stunned amazement as the head was followed by a shoulder and then a tiny arm and another shoulder. In a rush of fluid, the baby slipped from her womb and into Dr. Fleming's hands.

"Hello, little one. Happy birthday!" Dr. Fleming said, holding the baby up and wiping its face. "She wants to hold the baby and have skin-to-skin contact."

The baby made a little squeak, then began to cry.

"My baby!" Janet's eyes filled with tears, a rush of emotion overwhelming her as Dr. Fleming laid the baby on her chest. "My baby!"

She held the wet, squalling baby, Jack and the anesthesiologist tugging her hospital gown down to expose her breasts.

"Aren't you even going to look?" Dr. Fleming asked.

It took Janet a moment to understand what he meant. She lifted one of the baby's chubby legs and laughed. "It's a girl!"

Jack smiled at her, tears streaming down his face.

"Thank you, angel." He bent down, kissed her on the cheek, then kissed their little girl on her damp hair. "Welcome to the world, princess."

J ack sat close to the bed and watched as Janet tried to nurse Lily for the first time.

My God, he had a *daughter*.

He hadn't seen that coming.

They'd named her Lily Kathleen after Janet's mother and Jack's grandmother, but hadn't yet shared her name or sex with anyone.

Janet tickled the baby's chubby cheek with her nipple, and Lily turned her hungry little mouth toward Janet's breast, reminding Jack of a baby bird.

Janet gave a little gasp as the baby latched on and began to suck, then laughed, the happiness on her sweet face warming Jack to his soul.

"She's latched on really well all by herself," the nurse, a lactation specialist, said to Janet. "That's what we like to see."

Jack kissed Janet's cheek. "The kid's an expert already."

Janet turned to him. "Isn't she beautiful?"

She was the most beautiful thing he'd ever seen.

"Like mother, like daughter."

Janet didn't seem to be in pain. They'd given her some kind of narcotic injection through the epidural to relieve her pain while still enabling her to be alert so she could have bonding time with the baby. He hoped the pain relief lasted. He hated to think of her hurting. She'd been through enough.

It had been a long, hard pregnancy. Once she'd gotten through the nausea, she'd begun to have pain in her hip and pelvis. Jack had done everything he could think of to make her more comfortable—ice bags, hot compresses, massages, extra pillows. He'd brought in an acupuncturist recommended by Doc Johnson, who sometimes used acupuncture on the mares. None of it had completely taken away her discomfort, but she had soldiered through it.

Jack hadn't thought he could cherish her more than he had the day he'd married her, but watching her with Lily, he felt shaken by the depth of his love for her. He wanted to do right by her and Lily—and that meant he needed to talk to Nate.

Don't think about it now, amigo.

He reached over, took one of Lily's tiny hands between his fingers, almost unable to believe she was real. He laughed when the baby closed her entire hand around the tip of his pinky finger, he and Janet exchanging glances, both of them so lost in the baby that neither of them noticed when the nurse left the room.

There came a knock at the door.

Megan peeked her face inside. "Can we come in?"

"Please do," Janet answered.

Megan entered, carrying flowers, followed by Emily, who was dressed in a bright green sundress, and Nate, who was carrying little Jackson.

"Come here, Miss Emily." Jack got to his feet. "We have someone who really wants to meet you. This is Lily Kathleen."

Megan gave a little shriek. "A girl!"

"Congratulations to both of you!" Nate said, grinning ear to ear.

Emily approached the bed, a finger in her mouth, a shy smile on her face. She looked over at Lily. "Oh, Grandpa Jack, she's so pretty."

"You think so?" Jack sat, scooped Emily onto his lap.

Emily nodded, finger still in her mouth.

The girl had been acting out lately, no doubt feeling displaced by the new members of the family who were taking up so much of her parents' and Jack's time. They were doing all they could to make the transition easier for her, but she wouldn't adjust overnight. After all, she'd been the only child in the family for close to three years now and had gotten the lion's share of Jack's attention.

"Emily, this is Lily. Lily Kathleen, this is your niece, Emily." Janet looked from Lily to Emily. "She doesn't talk yet, but she'll learn. When she's done eating, you can hold her if you want."

Emily stared down at the baby. "Does she like me?"

"Are you kidding? She loves you," Jack answered. "So does Jackson. They're going to look up to you and need your help. You can teach them how to count, how to tie their shoes and—"

"I can teach them about horsies," Emily said, hopefully.

"That's what I was going to say next." Jack shared a smile with Megan and Nate. "They don't know a darned thing about horsies."

Megan put the flowers on the nightstand, sat down on the edge of the bed, and peered down at the baby. "Oh, she's just beautiful. Look at all that dark hair. How much did she weigh?"

"Seven pounds, thirteen ounces—a whole pound less than Jackson." Janet stroked Lily's downy hair.

"She takes after you, Janet," Megan said.

"Thank God for that," Jack joked.

He looked over at Nate. "Can we talk out in the hall?"

"Sure." Nate handed Jackson to Megan and followed him into the hallway, a look of concern on his face. "Is something wrong?"

"Not exactly." Jack didn't know how to say it except to come out and say it. "I'm sixty-four years older than that sweet little baby girl, and you and I both know it's unlikely that I'll be around to watch her turn thirty. I need to rewrite my will and make some provision for her. In the meantime, I want your promise that you'll do right by her and Janet if something happens to me before I get this all sorted out."

It wasn't going to be easy. The ranch needed to go to a single heir. Dividing it up between heirs would inevitably result in its being sold off piece by piece until it was no longer a viable operation, ending the family's legacy.

Nate raised an eyebrow. "I'm almost offended, Dad, but having a new baby shakes a man up, so I forgive you. Of course, I'll take care of Lily and Janet. Lily is my sister, and Janet is your wife, the woman you love. I would never throw either of them off the ranch, deprive them of monetary support, or leave them out of my will. I give you my word that they'll both have a home at the Cimarron for as long as they live."

Jack rested a hand on his son's shoulder, anxiety he hadn't realized he was carrying melting away. "Thank you, son. That means a lot to me."

"Now let's get back in there. I want to hold my baby sister." Nate grinned. "A girl. I'm amazed. That's the first West daughter in a century."

They went back into the room, where Janet was telling Megan about her C-section while Emily sat on the bed between them.

Lily had quit nursing and now seemed to be sound asleep.

Janet took the baby from her breast, drew her gown back up over her shoulder. "Okay, Emily, do you want to sit up here next to me?"

"Be careful." Jack helped Emily settle herself beside Janet. "Remember, they had to cut Janet's tummy open to get Lily out."

Janet laid Lily in Emily's arms. "Good job! You've gotten lots of practice holding babies, haven't you?"

There came a knock at the door, and the lactation nurse stepped in again. "It looks like the whole family is here. Hey, do you want me to get a picture?"

"That would be wonderful," Janet answered.

Nate took out his cell phone, handed it to the nurse, and showed her how to work it. "Just push the red button on the screen."

Nate went to stand beside Megan, who was holding Jackson, while Jack stood beside Emily, who still held Lily.

The nurse stepped back, took a few shots. "These look great."

"Thanks." Nate took the camera from her, scrolled through the images with a smile on his face, then handed his phone to Jack.

And there in color were the people Jack loved most in the world—and the second chance at happiness he'd never expected to have. He had no idea what tomorrow would bring or where life would take any of them. But right now, in this moment, everything was perfect.

They're beautiful.

Theresa's voice sounded inside his mind as if she were standing here beside him.

Yes, they are. I love them so much.

Could she hear him, too?

Be happy, my love.

And it seemed to Jack that Theresa was saying goodbye.

"Are you okay, hon?" Janet reached out, slid her fingers between his.

Jack swallowed the lump in his throat, gave his wife's hand a squeeze, his heart aching with the bittersweet wonder of life. "Never been better."

Keep reading for an excerpt from **Seduction Game** (I-Team 7), available in ebook format on October 20, 2015, and in print in March 2016 from Penguin Group (USA).

From *Seduction Game* (I-Team 7), coming Oct. 20, 2015, from Berkley!

CHAPTER ONE

*T*rust no one.

What the hell was Kramer trying to tell him?

Nick Andris rubbed his closed eyes with the heels of his hands, then looked up at the clock. Almost midnight.

Shit.

This was a waste of time.

For almost three weeks, he'd been keeping Holly Elise Bradshaw under round-the-clock surveillance. He'd turned her life inside out, but had found nothing. He'd tapped her cell phone and landline, sifted through her laptop, searched her condo, memorized the details of her childhood, learned about her friends, pored over her financial records, scrutinized her posts on social media for hints of tradecraft, and tracked every move she'd made via GPS. He'd found nothing remotely suspicious.

He'd even gone behind Bauer's back and contacted Rich Lagerman, an old buddy from Delta Force who was now working for the FBI, and asked whether Bradshaw was one of theirs. Every federal agency in the country now had undercover officers, and it wouldn't be the first time operatives from different agencies had tripped over one another while pursuing a suspect.

"Nope. Not one of ours," Lagerman had said. "But if you need any help with her, maybe some late-night, under-the-covers work, let me know."

"Right."

Nick now knew more about this woman now than she knew about herself. If Holly Bradshaw were some kind of underworld operative, a foreign agent, a traitor who sold US secrets, then he was Elvis fucking Presley.

Someone at Langley had screwed up.

Bauer had recalled Nick from assignment in Tbilisi amid whispers that a handful of officers were missing or dead and that the Agency was conducting an internal investigation of its Special Activities Division, or SAD, the top-secret branch of the CIA that had recruited Nick out of Delta Force nine years ago. He'd never been assigned to operate within US borders, so he'd arrived in Langley expecting to find himself in the middle of an inquisition.

Instead, Bauer, his supervisor, had given him a file with the latest intel on Sasha Dudayev, aka Sachino Dudaev, the Georgian arms smuggler who'd killed the only woman Nick had ever loved.

"He killed an officer and stole a flash drive containing classified information vital to US operations outside the homeland," Bauer had said. "Holly Elise Bradshaw is his contact for the deal. Keep Bradshaw under surveillance, recover the data, and neutralize them both using any force necessary."

As a rule, the Agency left affairs within the homeland to the NSA and FBI, but they sometimes broke that rule when it came to high-value international targets and US citizens who'd crossed the line to work with those targets. It was unusual for Nick to run surveillance on a fellow

American in her home, but apart from that element of his current mission, Bauer had given him exactly what he'd wanted for two long years now—a chance to make Dudaev pay.

Dudaev had played the Agency and brought the Batumi op down on their heads. Nick had been there that night. He'd watched, wounded and pinned down by AK fire, as the son of a bitch had emptied his Makarov into Dani's chest, then made off with the cache of AKs the Agency had wrested away from Chechen terrorists. Nick had crawled over to Dani and held her body afterward, held her until he'd passed out from blood loss.

His sole task that night had been to protect her, and he'd failed.

But now things were about to come full circle.

There was only one problem.

The suits at Langley had clearly made a mistake when they'd fingered Ms. Bradshaw as Dudaev's contact. Okay, so it was an understandable error. The bastard's last lover had been an Italian journalist who'd acted as his mole and messenger—until he'd had her killed. Analysts must have assumed he'd recruited Ms. Bradshaw when she'd interviewed him about his new art gallery and then begun dating him.

As understandable as the error might be, nothing changed the fact that Nick had now wasted *three weeks* discovering that Holly Bradshaw was exactly what she seemed to be—an entertainment writer, a smart but shallow blonde, a woman who loved sex, expensive clothes, and good times with her friends. He'd explained all of this to Bauer, sharing every bit of intel he'd gathered on her. If Dudaev was about to sell the flash drive, the deal would go down without Bradshaw's knowledge or participation.

Bauer had blown him off. "Stick with her. I swear she's the one."

Some people just hated to be wrong.

Nick's time would be better spent trailing Dudaev and hunting down the real contact—or sorting truth from rumor on the internal investigation and the missing and dead officers.

Trust no one.

Kramer had contacted him this afternoon, insisting they speak face to face. He'd be passing through Denver tomorrow and had asked Nick to meet him for lunch. Nick hadn't needed to ask what was on Kramer's mind. It wasn't unusual for an officer to be killed in the line of duty, but it *was* strange that Nick and Kramer had worked with all of them. Then Kramer had ended the call with those three words—and Nick's imagination had taken over.

"They're ombré crystal pumps in royal blue with four-inch heels."

Nick took another swig of cold coffee. In his earpiece, Bradshaw and her friend Kara McMillan were *still* talking.

"I love them," Bradshaw said, "but my shoe budget is blown for the next ten years."

Nick doubted that. Bradshaw's daddy was a retired brigadier general who had served with US Army Intelligence—another reason analysts believed Dudaev had chosen her—and Daddy had created a nice little trust fund for his baby girl.

"How much do a pair of Christian Louboutins cost?" McMillan asked.

Nick ran through the key facts on McMillan, more to help himself stay awake than because he'd forgotten anything.

McMillan, Kara. 40. Journalist, author, journalism instructor at Metro State University. Wife of Sheridan, Reece, lieutenant governor of the state of Colorado. No arrests. No suspected criminal associations. Three children. Formerly employed by the Denver Independent *on its*

Investigative Team, aka, the I-Team. Met Bradshaw through work. Close personal friend.

"Well, it depends on where you buy them, whether they're on sale, which shoe you choose—that sort of thing."

"Holly," McMillan said in a stern voice. "How much?"

Bradshaw hesitated. "These were just over three thousand."

Nick had just taken another swig of coffee and nearly choked.

Three thousand *dollars?* For a fucking pair of shoes?

"Wow!" McMillan laughed. "Reece would divorce me."

Damn straight!

"Did you get them for your big date with Sasha tomorrow?"

"I needed something to go with my new dress."

Nick rolled his eyes. The woman's closet was full of shoes. The last thing she needed was one more pair—especially one that cost *three fucking grand.*

"I read in the paper that he's a billionaire—gas and oil money," McMillan said.

Nick's jaw clenched.

Dudaev had built his fortune on human lives, including Dani's. Killing her had been nothing more than a business transaction to him. He could change his name, wear designer suits, and open a dozen art galleries to make himself seem respectable, but nothing could wash the blood off his hands.

"You should see the sapphire necklace he gave me last week. The chain isn't actually a chain. It's a strand of diamonds."

Nick already knew from another conversation—this time with Sophie Alton-Hunter, another friend from the newspaper—that Bradshaw had bought the dress to match the necklace. Now she'd gotten the shoes to go with the dress. And at last Nick understood what a woman like Holly Bradshaw would see in Dudaev.

Well, greed was blind.

She had no idea what kind of man he truly was. If she wasn't careful, he'd strangle her with that necklace.

"Sophie told me. It sounds like he's serious about you. Do you think this will be it—the big night?"

Nick frowned.

What did McMillan mean by that?

"I don't know. I mean, he's good looking enough."

"Good looking enough?" McMillan laughed. "He's a lot better looking than that banker you went out with last year. Where was he from?"

"South Africa."

"He's better looking than that Saudi prince, too, whatever his name was. In the news photos, he looks a lot like George Clooney. Sure, he's got some gray, but I'll bet he's fully functional."

Ah, yes. They were talking about Ms. Bradshaw's love life. Again.

Nick glanced for a moment at the photos of her he'd pinned to the wall above his desk. He could see why men were eager to sleep with her. She *was* hot.

Okay, she was incredibly hot. Platinum blond hair. A delicate, heart-shaped face. Big brown eyes. A full mouth, and a body that...

Get your mind off her body.

What good were looks if they got you into trouble? There were men who preyed on beautiful women, and Dudaev was one of them.

"Yeah, but he's... I don't know... self-absorbed. He's probably the kind of man who makes you wish you had a magazine to read when you're in bed with him. You know—the kind who acts like he's doing you a big favor when he rams into you for two minutes."

McMillan was laughing now.

But Bradshaw hadn't finished. "A lot of guys are oblivious like that. 'Don't worry about getting me off, babe. I just want to go down on you all night long'—said no man ever."

Nick shook his head. Is that truly what she expected?

A dude would have to have a motorized tongue to pull that off.

Did all women talk like this about sex? Nick couldn't imagine his sister sharing details about her sex life with her friends or using this kind of language. His mother, a devout Georgian Orthodox Christian, would have had a coronary if she'd caught her daughter or even one of her five sons talking like this.

Not that it offended Nick. He found it kind of sexy, actually. But then, given the things he'd seen and the things he'd had to do, a conversation about oral sex was pretty damned tame.

"Not all men are selfish."

You tell her, McMillan.

"No, I suppose not. But lots of them are. It makes me want to take out a full-page ad in the paper just to help out womankind. 'It's the clit, stupid.'"

Nick let out a laugh—then caught himself.

Keep your shit together, Andris.

Holly Bradshaw glanced over her shoulder at her living room wall. "Mr. Creeper must be watching something funny on TV. I just heard him laugh. I never hear him."

"You still haven't met him?" Kara asked through a yawn.

"He's lived there for almost a month now and hasn't once come over to say hello. He stays indoors and keeps the shades drawn. I've seen him outside once. He was taking out the trash, but he was wearing a hoodie. I couldn't see his face."

Kara's voice dropped to a whisper. "Maybe he's a serial killer."

"You're *not* helping."

"Who cares about him anyway? If I were you, I'd be so excited about tomorrow night. You lead such a glamorous life. I'm so jealous."

But Holly knew that wasn't true. "You and Sophie and the others— you spend every evening with your kids and men who love you, while I watch TV by myself or go out to the clubs. I think you're the lucky ones."

Like the rest of Holly's friends, Kara was happily married to a man who cherished her. Reece was one of the kindest, most decent, and sexiest men Holly had ever met—which was really strange, given that he was a politician. He'd bent over backward to prove to Kara that he loved her. Now, they had three kids and lived what seemed to Holly to be a perfect life.

The fact that all of her friends were now married and most had children had changed her life, too. She spent a lot less time out on the town with them and a lot more time alone while they took on new roles and responsibilities. As much as she loved excitement and enjoyed the city's nightlife, a part of her had begun to long for what they had—a family, a sense of roots, the certainty of belonging with someone. If she hated anything more than boredom, it was loneliness.

But Kara didn't seem to believe her. "Are you saying you'd be willing to trade places with me?"

"And sleep with Reece?" Holly smiled to herself, stretched out on her sofa, and wiggled her toes.

"That's not what I meant."

But the question, however intended, had Holly's imagination going.

Reece was sexy with dark blond hair, blue eyes and muscles he hid beneath tailored suits. How fun it would be to peel one of those suits away from his skin.

Then there was Julian Darcangelo, Tessa's husband. He was the city's top vice cop and a former FBI agent who'd worked deep cover. Tall with shoulder-length dark hair, a ripped body, and a strikingly handsome face, he was sex on a stick—and crazy in love with his wife.

Then again, Marc Hunter, Sophie's husband, had served six years in prison and had that badass vibe Holly loved. A former Special Forces sniper, he was also devoted to his family—and sexier than any man had a right to be.

Gabe Rossiter, Kat James's husband, had a rock climber's lean, muscular build and a daredevil attitude. He had all but given his life for the woman he loved. Kat was a lucky woman.

Zach McBride, a former Navy SEAL and Medal of Honor recipient, had saved Natalie from being murdered by the leader of a Mexican drug cartel. All lean muscle and confidence, he had the hard look of a man who was used to taking action.

Nate West, Megan's husband, had been badly burned in combat, his face and much of his body disfigured. The part of him that wasn't scarred was extremely handsome—and he had a cowboy charm that brought the song "Save a Horse (Ride a Cowboy)" to Holly's mind.

Javier Corbray had rescued his wife, Laura Nilsson, from captivity in a terrorist stronghold in Pakistan, sacrificing his career as a SEAL. With a sexy Puerto Rican accent, dreamy, dark eyes and a mouth that—

"Are you fantasizing about my husband?" Kara's accusing voice jerked Holly out of her reverie.

"No, of course not. Not really. Okay, a little," Holly confessed. "I was just deciding which one of you I'd most like to trade places with."

It was just a game. Holly had never so much as flirted with a married man. She didn't poach on other women's territory. But that didn't mean she couldn't fantasize.

"Holly!" Kara laughed. "I'm sorry I phrased it the way I did. Let me try again."

Tessa, Holly decided.

She'd trade places with Tessa. She'd always had a secret crush on Julian.

But Kara went on. "If you want to meet good men, maybe you should quit going to the clubs. Most of the guys there are just looking for someone to hook up with."

It wasn't the first time Kara had suggested this, but she didn't understand.

How could she?

Holly fired back. "You met Reece at a bar."

Okay, so it had been a restaurant. Still, Kara had consumed three margaritas, so it might as well have been a bar.

"Only because *someone* interfered," Kara replied.

Holly smiled to herself. It had been *so* easy.

"Where else can a woman meet men? If I don't go out, I'll never meet anyone. It's not like Mr. Right is going to just walk up and knock on my front door."

"You never know." Kara changed the subject. "Hey, did you hear that Tom is converting to Buddhism?"

Holly sat upright. "Tom? The same Tom Trent I know? The one who spends his day shouting at everyone? He's converting to *Buddhism*?"

"That's what my mother says."

Kara's mother Lily lived with Tom.

"She would know. But Tom—a Buddhist? He and the Dalai Lama have *so* much in common, like, for example … nothing."

Tom was the editor-in-chief of the *Denver Independent*, where his temper was as much of a legend as his journalistic brilliance. As an entertainment writer, Holly didn't work directly beneath him like her I-Team friends did. Beth Dailey, the entertainment editor, was her boss. Beth never yelled, never insulted people—and she appreciated Holly's shoes.

"I think it's perfect," Kara said. "If anyone needs to meditate, it's Tom. Gosh, it's after midnight. I need to get to bed—and so do you if you want to be rested for tomorrow night."

The two said good night and ended the call.

Holly got up from the sofa and went through her nightly routine, undressing, brushing her teeth, and washing and moisturizing her face, a sinking feeling stealing over her. Naked, she walked over to her dresser and carefully took her new Louboutins out of their red silk bag, moving them in the light to make the crystals sparkle.

She didn't want to spend another moment with Sasha Dudayev, but she'd already accepted and had the shoes…

Just one more date and that would be it.

She tucked the shoes carefully back in the bag, turned out her light, and crawled between her soft cotton sheets.

*N*ick *fell to the floor, pain knocking the breath from him. He looked down, saw that the round had penetrated his right side. He pressed his hand against the wound to staunch the blood loss.*

He glanced over his left shoulder, caught sight of Dani. She lay flat on the ground behind a forklift, her gaze on him, her eyes wide.

She was safe.

Thank God!

She got to her knees, clearly about to run to him.

Nick shook his head in warning. "Stay there!"

But their attackers had already spotted her and opened fire again.

Rat-at-at-at-at!

AK rounds struck the forklift, ricocheting wildly.

Dani felt flat again, panic in her eyes.

Then Dudaev appeared, gliding down the center of the warehouse like an apparition.

The bastard walked over to Dani.

"No!" Nick shouted.

Dudaev glanced his way, looked back down at Dani and said something. Then he drew a Makarov from a shoulder holster inside his jacket.

"Dani! No!" Nick fought to reach her, bullets raining from above, pain and blood loss making it impossible to move.

He was too late.

God, no!

"Dani!"

Bam! Bam! Bam!

Nick awoke with a gasp, sweat beaded on his forehead, a hand pressed to his side. There was no blood, pain only a memory.

Around him, the room was silent.

Another nightmare.

He rose, walked to the bathroom, splashed cold water on his face, his sense of terror slowly receding, grief taking its place.

Dani.

Every damned time he had one of these, it was like losing her again, the pain as real and new as it had been when he'd lain there holding her body, her lifeless eyes looking up at him, her blood and his mingling on that warehouse floor.

God, how he wished it had been him.

How he wished Dudaev had killed him instead.

"They say they've got more leg room, but that's bullshit. I'm six feet. You just can't get leg room in economy."

Nick nodded, took a swig of Tsingtao, his gaze on Kramer as he typed a message onto the Notes app of Nick's phone with one finger. Nick had known Kramer since the beginning. He'd been working under Bauer when Nick had joined the Agency and had taken Nick under his wing, acted as his mentor, showed him the ropes.

Kramer had always seemed indestructible to Nick, but today he was looking rough around the edges—older, pale, worn. There were thick bags under his eyes and a couple of days of whiskers on his jaw. His hair was more gray than brown now and looked as if it hadn't been combed in a few days. Then again, he'd just flown in from South Korea. But it was more than that.

For the first time since Nick had known him, Kramer seemed shaken, worried.

Kramer turned the phone so Nick could read it.

`We've got big trouble.`

As soon as he'd read the message, Nick deleted it and typed his own.

`An internal investigation. Who? Why?`

"I'm six-three, man," he said aloud. "You're preaching to the choir."

On his plate, an order of kung pao beef was growing cold, the food and conversation nothing more than cover.

Kramer frowned, took the phone, typed.

`Daly, Carver, both dead.`

"I sat there for the last three hours of the flight wishing I could stash my legs in the overhead compartment," Kramer went on, the tone of his voice casual, his Brooklyn accent standing out in this crowd of Coloradans and California imports.

"I've had that same fantasy." Nick deleted the words, typed his own message.

`I heard. Were they outed?`

Kramer shrugged, deleted Nick's message, and began to type again. "They're going to have to decrease their fares or take out a couple of rows of seats if I'm ever going to climb into one of their rust buckets again. I felt like a goddamn sardine."

`McGowen's dead, too.`

"Too bad you've still got four hours of flying time to go, old buddy." Nick's mouth formed words that barely registered with his mind as he did the mental math, a sense of foreboding growing in his gut.

He typed out his reply.

`They were all part of the Batumi op. What the hell is going on?`

"Yeah, too damned bad about that for sure." Kramer looked Nick straight in the eyes, typed one last message, then finished his beer and stood.

Nick turned the phone so that he could read it.

`Watch your six.`

That was it? Kramer had met with him just to tell him to watch his back?

Nick had every intention of doing just that, of course. He erased the message, stood. "Want a ride to the airport?"

Kramer tossed a couple bucks onto the table. "I'll grab a cab."

As he watched Kramer leave the little Chinese joint, Nick felt certain that Kramer knew more about all of this than he'd just shared.

Copyright © 2015 Pamela Clare

ALSO BY PAMELA CLARE

Romantic Suspense

I-Team Series

Extreme Exposure (Book 1)

Heaven Can't Wait (Book 1.5)

Hard Evidence (Book 2)

Unlawful Contact (Book 3)

Naked Edge (Book 4)

Breaking Point (Book 5)

Skin Deep: An I-Team After Hours Novella (Book 5.5)

First Strike: The Prequel to Striking Distance (Book 5.9)

Striking Distance (Book 6)

Soul Deep: An I-Team After Hours Novella (Book 6.5)

Seduction Game (Book 7)

Dead by Midnight: An I-Team Christmas (Book 7.5)

Contemporary Romance

Colorado High Country Series

Barely Breathing (Book 1)

Historical Romance

Kenleigh-Blakewell Family Saga

Sweet Release (Book 1)

Carnal Gift (Book 2)

Ride the Fire (Book 3)

MacKinnon's Rangers series

Surrender (Book I)

Untamed (Book 2)

Defiant (Book 3)

Upon A Winter's Night: A MacKinnon's Rangers Christmas (Book 3.5)

ABOUT THE AUTHOR

USA Today best-selling author Pamela Clare began her writing career as a columnist and investigative reporter and eventually became the first woman editor-in-chief of two different newspapers. Along the way, she and her team won numerous state and national honors, including the National Journalism Award for Public Service. In 2011, Clare was awarded the Keeper of the Flame Lifetime Achievement Award. A single mother with two sons, she writes historical romance and contemporary romantic suspense at the foot of the beautiful Rocky Mountains. To learn more about her or her books, visit her website at www.pamelaclare.com. You can keep up with her on Goodreads, on Facebook, or search for @Pamela_Clare on Twitter to follow her there.

Made in the USA
Lexington, KY
06 August 2017